Holly C. Wyse

The
RESTORATION
OF EMMA CARMICHAEL

A Novel

THE RESTORATION OF EMMA CARMICHAEL
Copyright © 2013 by Holly C. Wyse

Scripture taken from the Holy Bible, NEW INTERNATIONAL VERSION®. Copyright © 1973, 1978, 1984, 2011 by Biblica, Inc. All rights reserved worldwide. Used by permission. NEW INTERNATIONAL VERSION® and NIV® are registered trademarks of Biblica, Inc. Use of either trademark for the offering of goods or services requires the prior written consent of Biblica US, Inc. • Scripture quotations marked (NLT) are taken from the Holy Bible, New Living Translation, copyright 1996. Used by permission of Tyndale House Publishers, Inc., Wheaton, Illinois 60189. All rights reserved. • Scripture quotations from The Message. Copyright © by Eugene H. Peterson 1993, 1994, 1995, 1996, 2000, 2001, 2002. Used by permission of NavPress Publishing Group.

ISBN: 978-1-77069-791-1

Word Alive Press
131 Cordite Road, Winnipeg, MB R3W 1S1
www.wordalivepress.ca

Library and Archives Canada Cataloguing in Publication
Wyse, Holly C., 1979-
    The restoration of Emma Carmichael / Holly C. Wyse.
ISBN 978-1-77069-791-1
    I. Title.

PS8645.Y83R47 2013   C813'.6   C2012-908462-X

For Jesus, My Rock and Redeemer.

Acknowledgements

First, I would like to thank Word Alive Press for the wonderful opportunity to become a published author. Your support and belief in this story have meant so much to me. I am forever grateful for the time, effort, design, creativity, money, and resources that have gone into making this book a reality. Thank you so very much.

To my ninja editor, Evan Braun. Thank you for believing in this story and believing in me even when I wanted to give up on myself and bring in zombies to hasten the ending. Where would Emma be without you—literally, where? I appreciate your sharp eye, your skill with the red pen, your grammar finesse, and all the long (and late!) hours you put into this project. You are a ninja!

Thank you to my family for all their support while I wrote this book. I love you.

My dear friend, Lisa Eirich, the first person to read a handful of pages and encourage me by saying, "Send me the next three chapters." Thank you for your belief.

Jenny McQueen, my best pal, who endured three months of emails, texts, and conversations about imaginary people as I fine-tuned this book. Thank you for the Photoshop Beauty Treatment you did on my back cover photo; your mad skills are outta this world! I can always count on you for the truth.

Clarke Schroeder. Dude! Promise made, promise paid. You are, officially, a character… in my book. Tell your friends.

Tammy Adams and Kim Lavigne graciously shared with me their stories of self-injury, recovery, and the role self-injury plays in a person's life years later. Thank you for your transparency, honesty, and bravery. I am forever grateful that God brought our paths together.

Thank you to the fabulous Lolo B, Lisa and Katherine Friesen, Jeff and Ann Nemeth, David A. Poulsen, Angela Williams, Nikki Waugh, Jennifer Friesen, Bishop Ron Kuykendall, and Dr. Robert Simpson and his lovely wife, Trinh—all of whom did at least one of the following: provided information used in this book, watched my children for me so that I could meet my deadlines, prayed, prayed, and prayed.

Heartfelt thanks to Bishop Todd Atkinson, for speaking truth into my life and believing in my calling. Thank you for being my friend. And for wearing sweater vests.

To The Sister Club and Jeff and my Mama.

Amy, Lori Ann, and Jefferoo, you are the best hooligans a girl could grow up with. Any scenes that reflect our real-life conversations or your high school diary entries (Jeff) are merely coincidence. Mom, thank you for teaching me to worship Jesus in the dark times, to obey God even when it's uncomfortable, and for the fervent belief that my penchant for telling tall tales would eventually be turned around for good.

I want to honour the memory of two incredible souls who impacted me greatly. My wonderful father, Wil, who in his few years taught me about the Father heart of God and the power of forgiveness. And to my Gigi, Toini Isotalo, who taught me to dance… and to spell. Most of my memories of them are when they were laughing.

"Geologists have a saying: Rocks remember."
—Neil Armstrong

Chapter One

I changed my name when I was sixteen. I was tired of it.

It means *stone.*

As in, rock. The type of stone that is submerged in a river. Water and life flow around it, bubbling downstream, heading for adventure. Yet the rock stays, embedded in the mud, lodged in place.

I hate that name. I hate what it says about me.

Not many people know the meaning, but I do. And every time someone called me by that name, they were telling me something I already knew—that I was stuck.

It seems you can't escape your own destiny, even if you try to change it. Even if you tell everyone you have a new name. No matter what I do, I remain entrenched in the mud.

————

"Are you firing me?"

The words fall from my mouth heavy with realization. I sway slightly in front of the mahogany desk, hands hanging like wilted lilies.

"In a word… yes," the squat powerhouse says. Her brunette head bobs in front of me and she leans forward in her chair. Tapping her fingers together, my boss confirms my new reality. "I am firing you."

My blonde curls stick to the nape of my neck. It's only because there's no air conditioning in the room, not because I've broken out into a panic sweat.

"But I'm family," I protest. "I'm your niece!"

Aunt Cindy stands up, clucking her tongue and waving her finger. "Now, Emma, don't try playing that card. Or I'll play this card: I gave you this job as a favour to my sister."

"My mother got me this job?" My eyes widen as I realize something that should have been obvious from the start. "But you said—"

"Emma, what I said and what you wanted to believe are two different things."

I open my mouth to speak, but Aunt Cindy holds up a hand, commanding silence as she walks in front of her desk. This Lethbridge office is home to a monthly magazine representing the smaller communities of southern Alberta, but my aunt treats it like it's a big city business. Her grey power suit says so.

"You can't fire me. I'm still new. I'm learning." A yapping Chihuahua begging for a treat has more dignity than I do at the moment.

Folding her arms, Aunt Cindy leans back against the desk and sucks in her cheeks. She does that whenever she's growing impatient but needs to stay calm. Five weeks here has taught me that and not much else.

"No, Emma. You aren't new. Afif," Aunt Cindy points at a young man who is diligently typing at a computer, "is new. He's been here what... four days?"

More like three weeks.

"And he's moved from getting me coffee to working the Bird Watch column. You've been here almost two months and I'm still waiting for the back issues I requested two weeks ago."

"I'm getting to that." I fidget with my skirt and try not to chew on my bottom lip.

"And the layout requests Norman sent out this morning... are they ready for the one o'clock meeting?"

"Um... they will be? I mean, yes. Absolutely. They will be."

"And my coffee, where is it?"

Thanks a lot, Afif. You get promoted and I get java duty.

"Emma, I love you. You know that." Do I? "But your work ethic isn't worth the two-dollar shoes you're wearing."

I study my feet. Suddenly, my ten-dollar find at the Bargain Barn no longer seems like the success story I once thought it was.

"I can't keep covering for you," she says. "Listen, I know things have been rough since everything with Steven—"

Ben. His name is Ben.

"—but you have to move on. And you can't make excuses or hide behind things like 'I'm new.' Afif is the *new* new, and look what he's capable of."

Afif is a storm of activity. His fingers are speedily typing while he talks on the phone, and he still finds the time to flirt with the girl in the next cubicle. I hope he and his ambition get saddled with coffee duty once I leave.

A brown box is shoved into my hands. I'm mortified at everything the box signifies. My twenty-three years of life have led me to a series of dead ends. I'm like a child movie star who has hit puberty—all doors are locked and no one is taking my calls.

I'm stuck.

My aunt presses the intercom button on her phone. "Afif, can you please come in here regarding the matter I discussed earlier?"

I spy the paper shredder behind her desk. The thin wisps of paper cling together in a vain attempt to recall their former state. Once whole, they now hang detached, several pieces about to drop to the bottom of the wastebasket. I feel a deep and abiding connection to the dissected paper at this particular moment.

Afif stands in front of me without emotion, waiting to escort me out of the building.

"Ready to go, Emma?"

I look at my aunt once again.

"That will be all." She shuffles some papers, then adds, nonchalantly, "See you Sunday at Gigi and Papa's for dinner."

———

Flipping my phone open, I hit speed dial 2. I juggle the box containing the remnants of my life: a plethora of stationary and pens, a dying plant, and an unopened copy of *The Seven Habits of Highly Effective People*.

"Hi Emma," the voice huffs in my ear.

I smile. My sister, Natalie, is answering the phone while chasing one of her kids.

"Hi." My voice is small.

"What's wrong?"

"I just got fired."

"Aunt Cindy fired you?"

"Yeah."

"Why?"

"It wasn't working out."

I hear a sigh like a slow balloon leak. "That's too bad, Emma. I know this is the second job for you."

Third, actually. But I don't really count the time I worked at the farmer's market. It was, after all, only one day.

"What's going on?"

I set the box on top of my little blue Toyota and search for the keys. Natalie's question buzzes around my head, demanding an answer.

Groaning as I get into the car, I wish for the umpteenth time that Ben had fixed the air conditioning like he had promised. "Listen, Nat, I'm going home. Don't worry about me, I'll be fine."

"I'll call you later."

And I'll let it go to voicemail.

"I know you, Emma. Don't wallow on the couch listening to Johnny Cash songs and stuffing your face with chocolate marshmallow sandwiches," Natalie says.

"I'm not allowed to be depressed?"

"Sad, yes. Depressed, no. Don't worry, Emma. You'll find your place."

I sniff, fighting off tears.

"You will."

No, I won't. I don't have a place. I'm unwanted.

"Emma, trust me. You will. You just have to—"

Ugh. Not another one of my sister's rah-rah speeches. Who has time to listen to all this motivational mumbo-jumbo? Well, I guess I do. I have loads of time now.

"I'll talk to you later, Natalie." I close my phone and ignore the pang of guilt I feel over cutting my sister off.

I need a soundtrack for this horrible moment in my life. Cranking up some country music, I salute the building and shout, "Sayonara!"

I speed out of my parking spot, resolved to leave before I start crying.

Through the rear-view mirror, I spot my box of things fly off the roof of the car and scatter on the road behind me. I couldn't care less.

Chapter Two

Chocolate-covered bran bars, rainbow-coloured toothpaste, and strawberry-flavoured cough medicine all use marketing for a fresh spin to cover up their boring image and make them look like something they aren't. That's why I tell myself I'm going back to *my place*. My little home sweet home. It's the only way I can ignore the fact that it's really the glorified basement suite in my dad's house. Denial is a better option than the bitter truth of moving back in with my dad after my life imploded like a failed ad campaign for citrus-scented butt ointment. Somehow admitting that seems to say that I can't take care of myself, that I haven't grown up.

Of course, the giant stuffed teddy bear on my couch could convey the same message.

Dumping my purse and keys onto the counter, I wash my hands and tug at the fridge door. The cool air offers little consolation to my busy mind. Fatigued, I shut the door and collapse onto the couch.

The giant teddy bear comes in handy as something to hug. I really need a hug right now.

The home phone rings. It's probably just a pity call from some prying family member. They can leave a message on my old-school answering machine, another Bargain Barn find. It's a brilliant way to screen the calls I have no intention of returning.

The only connections I'm willing to have through my new cell phone are with Natalie (who lends a soft shoulder to cry on) and my best friend, Katie (who gives me swift kicks to the butt). I need both on a regular basis.

The large masses of people I used to text daily have gone the way of my old cell phone. Deleted and gone. After Ben's final message to me two months ago, I threw that phone away. I never wanted to see it again.

The machine whirs to life and my dad's voice announces, "Hey Emma, it's me."

I race for the phone. My dad has been in Nicaragua for a week and a half and I miss him like crazy.

"Daddy!" I grip the phone like it's the last pair of Lululemon pants on the rack.

"Hey, Emma. How are you? Have you been cutting the grass like you promised?"

I pause. The lawnmower hasn't moved in a week.

"Emma?"

"I was fired today."

"Aunt Cindy fired you?"

"Yeah."

"What happened?"

I'm as silent as the lawnmower in the garage. Should I tell him I can't hold down a job anymore? Does he suspect that I'm coming apart at the seams? Would he understand how insulted I am that Aunt Cindy thinks I would actually wear two-dollar shoes to work?

"Nothing."

"Emma?" His tone is familiar. If he were here, he'd be looking me in the eye with one eyebrow cocked. He used to be a big business kind of guy. He doesn't take excuses.

"I'm just a mess, Dad. I can't hold a job right now. I can't focus on anything but what I've lost. I keep thinking about what I was supposed to be doing with my life—like painting bedrooms and hanging pictures, fighting about toilet paper rolls and which way they're supposed to go on. But all that changed when the wedding was cancelled."

My father is silent. Is he remembering the bill for the non-refundable catering he paid for? Or is he creating a strategy for getting me a desk job at a friend's company?

"Hmmmm," is his only response. He's thinking. He's a solver, a doer, which is why he's in Nicaragua right now—building houses and helping locals start microbusinesses.

"Emma, I think you should just take it easy."

Am I hearing him correctly? Perhaps the connection from Managua is scrambling his words. This solution can't have come from the same man who made me dress up as a giant hot dog for a church fundraiser at age fourteen.

"Dad?"

"I think you should take it easy." I hear children laughing in the background. "Listen, I was worried about you when…"

Ben. He means Ben.

Neither of us say his name; we aren't really sure what will happen to me if his name is spoken. It's like his name is a bomb and speaking it will make it explode.

"…I didn't want you sliding back to the age of sixteen."

Oh, *that*. That's a landmine all its own.

"I pushed you. I wanted you working, doing something. I had hoped it would give you something else to look at."

"Dad, it was a good idea. Really. It got me out of bed each morning. I needed that. I still do. I need to get a new job."

"Maybe. I think you need some time, though. Take a few weeks off, maybe longer. Slow down. Heal."

I start to protest.

"Emma, you forget that I know what it's like to have the love of your life break your heart beyond ruin."

He means my mother. This hits like a weapon of mass destruction.

"I buried myself in work, remember?" he says.

I recall his absence. He hadn't been able to work long enough hours to keep away the pain. I'd spent lonely, dark months with a stoic father who came home late and left early.

"It didn't work, Emma. It only put time between me and the day she left."

He's silent for a moment. I know he's trying to make a point. I *have* put time between my jilted wedding day and me. Quite frankly, two months hasn't been enough.

"Emma, if you don't slow down, you aren't going to heal. I should know."

"There are bills to pay, Dad."

He chuckles. It's ridiculous to think that my measly rent is really covering the expenses of his house. It's futile to fight him. It didn't work when I wanted out of that bright red Oscar Meyer unitard, and it won't work now.

"Dad, I have a car that needs gas. I need to eat."

"That's what Daddy's credit card is for."

"No way. I'm not putting you into debt because I can't hold it together."

"Use my card. Eat nachos, get takeout, buy that green salad stuff you're always devouring. I've had dental work that has cost more than you can possibly spend."

"I'm twenty-two, Dad. I can't mooch off you."

"You aren't mooching if I'm giving you the freedom to take the next six weeks or two months to figure life out."

"Only six weeks, huh?"

"Look who's wanting more time," he teases.

I think about the possibility of trying to sort my heart out. "I have to be intentional about this, don't I?"

"I'm not going to make you do anything you aren't ready for, Emma. I'm saying, take some time to slow down. I've got it covered."

Without wanting it, my eyes fill with tears. I don't deserve kindness from my dad. He has already put up with so much loss because of me.

"I gotta go, Dad."

"I love you, Emma. Use my credit card and don't worry about it."

Choking back a sob, I manage a meagre but grateful "Thank you" before saying goodbye.

Hanging up the phone, the emotions of the last two months claw at my eyes and throat. They are heavy and thick, like a rope around my neck. I want to be free of them.

I race upstairs towards the garage and pull out the lawn mower. I need something loud enough to drown out my thoughts.

I need something to cut.

Chapter Three

I'm on the couch covered by what feels like a thin layer of dust. It very well could be, for I've been atrophying here for two days. I'm still wearing the baggy clothes I changed into after getting home from work on Wednesday.

Which makes today Friday.

For some reason, that thought fires synapses and neurons in my brain. I have the vague sense that I'm supposed to do something. Or be somewhere.

My mind is filled with fog, like a harbour on a warm morning. It settles in my brain, rendering me unable to make a connection with reality.

I look at the ceiling and sigh. Why am I so alone?

The ceiling stares back at me with no answer.

Despondency.

Now that's a great word. I think I'll use it next time someone asks how I'm doing.

The urgency of the ringing phone revives me. I consider letting it go to the answering machine. A gnawing premonition makes me give in and pick up on the third ring.

"Where are you?" a voice hisses. "I've left ten messages on your cell phone."

Crumb.

"Katie. Hi!" I force enthusiasm into my voice. The fog starts to clear.

Heaving myself off the couch, I step on some wayward nacho chips and see my dead cell phone on the floor.

"Emma. You told me you would be here. You pinky-swore!"

Pushing my bedroom door open, I scan the messy floor for something clean to wear. I know things are in a bad way when smelling my clothes is the only way to conclude if they're passable for a public outing.

"Yeah, I'm on my way," I assure her.

I find an old blue V-neck that passes for semi-decent.

"Oh, you are not," she grunts. "Are you even dressed?"

"Yes." Well, technically I'm wearing clothes.

"But you aren't ready, are you?"

I chew on my lip, trying to think of an answer.

"Emma!"

"I'll be there. I said I'll be there, and I meant it."

"I bought the movie tickets because you said you would be here. I'm standing in line!" Another grunt comes across the line. "You know, Em, I liked it a lot better when you were the kind of best friend I could count on."

"And I prefer it when you don't grunt like a caveman to convey your annoyance. Katie, you know I'm going through a lot right now. You know that I'm—"

"I know, I know... mourning the future you thought you had."

"Katie, I think I might have depression."

Katie sighs. "You are sad. Life stinks right now. You're directionless, in a valley. You're a cliché."

I'm tempted to hang up. But I can't hang up on a friend who calls my many bluffs. Plus, she's put up with everything from my bad hair days to my current obsession with country music.

"I'll be there."

"It's a fifteen-minute drive and the movie starts in ten minutes. You better pray that your gas tank is full and you don't have to stop anywhere."

"Yes, Mother," I mock.

"Oh, shut it and get here!"

Hanging up, I yank on the V-neck, grab some fresh underwear, and pull on a pair of jeans to hide my unshaven legs. Running to the bathroom, I turn the faucet taps violently. Cool water splashes my shirt, creating a spreading wet spot.

There's no time to change. I decide to drive down the highway with the heater running full-blast to dry the shirt. I'm a genius! There's profound truth tucked into the old adage that says necessity is the mother of invention.

Dear God, Katie is right. I *am* a living cliché.

———

"I'm Dr. Martha Hunt and we're walking the walk today. Nancy from Baltimore, you are on the air."

"Hi, Dr. Martha. I love your radio show. Thank you for taking my call."

I apply eyeliner as I race down the highway. I push away the nagging worry that I might crash while holding a sharp object to my eye.

Nancy's voice quivers. "I think—well, I suspect—that, perhaps, my boyfriend and I may be breaking up."

"You think… suspect… perhaps? Nancy, you are all over the place. Do you want this relationship to end?"

"No! No, not at all, Dr. Martha. I love him. I want to marry him."

"Why do you think you're going to break up? Has he said anything?"

I lean forward and turn up the volume.

"Well, no. It's just that…" A sorrowful sigh fills the airwaves.

"Nancy?"

"Well, the other day I was on his Facebook page and—"

"Okay, stop right there."

Accelerating to five kilometres over the speed limit, I shout, "Go for the jugular, Dr. Martha!" I mean, really. Why call if this is just another Facebook fiasco?

"Nancy, are you phoning to tell me that you saw something he wrote, said, or made a comment on and you've assumed something about your relationship because of it?"

"It's not like that, you see—"

"Yes or no, Nancy."

A tiny "yes" squeaks out.

"Have you talked to him before you talked to me about this?"

"No."

"How many other people have you asked?"

"Only three."

"Amateur," I mutter, signalling to cross over onto the exit ramp.

"And how old are you, Nancy?"

"Twenty-one."

"Uh-huh. Nancy, if this is someone you truly believe you are going to marry one day, you're going to have to work on the concept of communication. A wise woman doesn't ask her girlfriends to interpret her man for her. She goes straight to him and says, 'Honey, I was on your Facebook page today and saw this. Can you tell me about it?' And then, Nancy, I want you to do this next step very carefully. Are you ready?"

"Yes."

"I want you to *listen*." The word is drawn out like a piece of bubblegum being stretched into string. "Don't talk, don't interrupt, don't think about your feelings. Just *listen*."

I pull into a parking lot and park next to a brown Suburban.

"What if his answer is lame or he lies to me?"

"Nancy, if you think he's going to lie to you over a Facebook comment, you're either insecure or you need to rethink your list of what makes a man marriage material."

"Oh."

"I'm Dr. Martha Hunt."

———

"You're leaving me, too?" I slump onto the bench with new thoughts of abandonment. Another piece of my heart breaks. The pain travels under my skin and settles in my arms.

"Look who's being dramatic." Katie adjusts her sunglasses into a makeshift headband as her Vietnamese features form a scowl.

"I'm not being dramatic. I just can't believe you're moving to Toronto."

And leaving me to navigate my post-Ben life all alone.

"Come on, Emma. You were going to get married and move away. I needed to do something to start my life."

"Why does everyone leave me?"

"No one is leaving you."

I look up and start a list. "Ben, my dad, you, my m—"

Katie laughs. "Spare me, Em. I don't count—I need to get a life. Toronto has the kind of dance community I want to be part of, and a lot of the Vietnamese side of my family lives there. Your dad doesn't count, either, because he had made plans to spend the summer in Nicaragua long before the wedding was cancelled, and Ben… well…" Any words of reason fade away on the wind. "The Emma I know would be happy for me."

"I am. Really, Katie, I am. The chance to work in Toronto has always been a dream of yours. You need to do it. It's just that…" I lose my words and look out at the park in front of us.

"Yeah, I know. Your heart is broken."

"Katie! How can you be so… so blasé about it?"

"Because it's all we talk about," Katie says. "You go off into this weird headspace and get a far-off look in your eyes."

"I happen to be deeply hurt."

"I'm well aware."

"Are you?"

Katie gives me a pointed look. "I'm also aware that if you don't start moving on, or at least moving, you're going to be stuck in this frame of mind for a long time. Maybe the rest of your life." She snaps her fingers. "I know! Let's go on a road trip. You can drive me to my aunt's place in Montana and we'll have one last hurrah before I leave."

My eyes narrow. "Hurrah?"

"A change of scenery is just what you need, Em." With a smile, she drops her sunglasses over her eyes. "Besides, this sad phase is doing nothing for your choice in clothes."

I stare at my blue shirt, its water stain no longer visible.

"Come on, that was supposed to be a joke."

"It wasn't funny," I say.

"Em, you can't camp out in this place of bitterness. You don't want to talk about God, but you need Him. He loves you and can turn this around."

"Katie, please stop placating me with bumper sticker slogans. Don't you understand? I'm wounded and gutted. I gave Ben my heart and he used a meat-cleaver on it. My heart is a tiny pile of bacon bits. God could have saved me from my salad-topping fate, but He didn't. I sought Him for direction. I asked Him for guidance and He led me here—to Broken-and-Woundedville!"

"You've been listening to too much country music." Katie stands up and grabs her purse. "I'm still going to pray for you, though."

She starts to leave. The invisible elastic band of friendship stretches between us. I hope it will spring back quickly and return Katie to the bench beside me.

Katie only turns and offers, "I leave in two weeks."

I watch as my so-called best friend heads to her car. Feeling the invisible band break, I stare numbly at the receding image.

Despondency…

Chapter Four

"**A**untie Emma!"

Oof! I receive a tackle from Jack, my four-year-old nephew. His usual means of greeting me includes a run at full speed followed by a flying leap that I, more often than not, am not prepared for.

"Hey, Jackie-man! How are you?"

My nephew thrusts out his hand. "Look at my new dinosaur! It's a velociraptor—that means thief swift." He squints his blue eyes against the bright sun and scrunches his nose. "No, that's not right. I mean swift thief."

"Very impressive," I say, turning over the brown plastic toy in my hand.

"Swift means fast, Auntie Emma. I'm fast. Watch!" Jack takes three quick steps down the sidewalk, then comes back. "Oh, I need my dinosaur."

I hand him his toy and laugh as he takes off towards his mom, whose arms hold Grace, my sleeping baby niece.

"I'm glad you decided to come," Natalie says as I follow Jack, albeit at a much slower pace. She shifts the baby and smooths her green tanktop and patterned skirt. Tucking her dark chin-length hair behind her ear, she warns Jack to slow down.

"Jackie, walk, don't run." His father's reprimand is harsh, yet warranted.

Natalie and I exchange a look. "Did you guys fight on the way here?"

Natalie shrugs. "It's just one of those days."

Her husband, Mark, is like an ocean wave about to crest. He takes a deep breath, trying to control his temper, then speaks more softly to their son. No doubt he's going over the finer points of good behaviour which are required at Gigi and Papa's monthly dinner.

The last Sunday of the month has always belonged to Gigi and Papa. My father stopped coming once he and my mother split, but he would faithfully drop us off and wave as we climbed the porch steps. Natalie and I would race to the top to see which one of us was first to ring the doorbell or press our noses against the glass door.

I'm tempted to dare Natalie to race me up the steps, but one glance at the baby in her arms reminds me that we aren't kids any more.

Just looking at the house fills me with warmth. Home. This is home for me now more than ever. I think that's why I chose to have my wedding here. That, and the stunning garden in the backyard.

"Emma!" The aroma of slow-cooked pork envelops me as my Papa opens the door in greeting.

Easing into my grandfather's arms, I breathe in the familiar scent of peppermint mixed with soil. His hands push me back. Holding me at arm's length, his grey eyes search my face. His shaggy brows rob the moment of its seriousness.

"Papa, I'm fine."

"Right. And your Uncle Fred hasn't started smoking again." He pats my hand and I try not to laugh. "This isn't the best time to *really* talk, Emma. You come by and see me during the week. We'll play chess."

Chess is our game. It's Papa's invitation to me, his way of saying that he wants to help me through this phase of my life. He taught me to play when my teenage heart was broken. My arms and hands needed to play a different game than the emotional one they were involved in.

"I don't know, Papa."

"What? No time for your Grandpa? We need to talk. I have—"

"Roarrr!" Jack bursts through the doorway with a force akin to a wild stampede.

Papa's shaggy eyebrows lift. Turning from me, his hand encircles Jack's wrist. Jack's eyes widen as my Papa lowers himself to Jack's level. His little body shifts nervously. Papa leans in. "Boo!"

"*Roaarrrr!*" Jack shouts back. He holds up his hands like claws and attacks Papa's shoulder.

I leave the entryway before I become T-Rex bait.

"We aren't eating for another twenty minutes," my cousin Andrea barks at me as I enter the dining room. "Oh, and I'm trying to focus. Don't start any annoying conversations with me."

Well, hello to you, too.

Hunched in a chair like a gnarled Joshua tree, she sits, madly texting someone. Her resolute posture resembles Aunt Cindy's.

But Andrea looks nothing like her mom, so at least there's that. This week, Andrea is wearing a bright pink wig. Her face is made up like one of her favourite anime characters, complete with fake eyelashes and contact lenses to give her the exaggerated wide-eyed look of a Japanese heroine. I half-expect floating subtitles to appear when she speaks.

Uncle Fred comes in and tries to nonchalantly join the group in the living room. We all pretend he hasn't been outside smoking.

"Emma, how wonderful to see you," a familiar voice greets me from the kitchen. "You're looking refreshed. I like that shirt on you, is it new?"

If my mouth would open, I could sass her with, "It's amazing how four days of no work and all play can restore a body." Instead, I just stare at Aunt Cindy.

Natalie to the rescue.

"Hi, Aunt Cindy. Did you just get your nails done?" My older sister is a mother bear to me. We treat it as a joke. In truth, the false laughter is a thin layer of ice separating us from the larger issue—an issue neither of us is willing to work through.

I feel a vibration in my pocket and pull out my cell phone. A text message from Katie reads: *Do you want some of my clothes and furniture? I can't move it all with me. Let me know, I'm trying to sort through all my stuff by Tuesday.*

Right, Katie's leaving. What or who is going to keep my company when she leaves? Her red IKEA rug?

I set my phone on the table and push it away. Andrea laughs at an Instagram photo, Natalie and Aunt Cindy compare cuticles, and Jack asks Uncle Fred why his mouth smells like a bonfire. Even though I'm surrounded by family, I feel utterly abandoned.

Chapter Five

"There you are." My Papa's kind voice interrupts my thoughts. "I've been looking you."

I'm in his study. The only friends I can count on are in this room—his books and chessboard. "It felt too crowded out there."

"I have something for you," he says.

He digs through the pockets of his grey slacks. Instantly I feel small again, hoping for a treat from my grandfather. To be truthful, even a handful of jujubes would help right now.

"Here it is." My grandfather keeps his hands around the hidden object and clears his throat. "I wanted to give you this, a symbol of sorts for new beginnings."

A symbol? Well, that rules out jujubes.

"I was praying for you this morning," he says. "I knew I needed to give you something to encourage you for the months ahead."

My insides warm. I picture my grandfather, sitting with his coffee and Bible in the armchair my Gigi thinks the study can do without.

He opens my hand and places a smooth river rock on my palm.

I blink. A stone? The unbelievable keeps happening to me. Katie is leaving, Papa is losing his mind, what's next? Carrie Underwood reveals that she's not a true blonde?

"Thank you, Papa," I manage.

"Can I share with you the story of this rock?"

"Okay." Maybe senility isn't taking over. Papa loves history. He loves stories, chronicles of the past that weave in wisdom and truth.

"Remember," he says, closing his eyes. "Our God tells us to remember. He instructs us to remember Him in all our ways, to recall and write down what He has done so that we don't forget His goodness and mercy. Do you remember how Abraham reminded himself of His encounter with the Most High?"

My mind tunnels through the annals of Bible history stuck in my brain. Haltingly I bring forth, "He built an altar?"

Papa lets the answer settle in. "Yes, he built an altar out of rocks. Why?"

"To remember."

"To remember what, Emma? What did Abraham not want to forget?"

"He didn't want to forget what God had done for him."

He wraps my fingers around the rock. "Yes. Exactly. You're on a journey now, Emma. You will recover." His eyes meet mine and hold a look of confidence. Then he shifts his gaze over my shoulder. "In fact, I think God will do more than recover you. I believe He's going to restore you."

His gaze is resting on Gigi's china cabinet in the dining room. The glass panes reflect the glow of the sun. Papa and I found it at an antique sale. He had thought it would be the perfect gift for Gigi—only it required a great deal of TLC. It took months of hard labour: stripping paint, sanding and refinishing, varnishing on Saturday afternoons rife with muttered threats of heaving it to the curbside. And yet here it stands, strong and ornately beautiful, grander than ever before, a noble chamber containing the most celebrated and precious pieces of our family history. It is unblemished.

Papa points to the cabinet. "You will be restored, Emma. And you will *know* it. And when it happens, you will want to remember what God has done for you. This stone is to mark the beginning of God's restoring work. Consider it your first stone in an altar of remembrance."

Suddenly, the rock feels weighted with meaning inside my hand.

"Dinner is about to get underway. I'll let them know you're coming."

Papa shuffles out of the room, stopping only to look at me when he reaches the china cabinet.

I stare at the rock in my hands. There's a scripture notation written on it in Papa's slanting stroke—Exodus 20:24.

Is my grandfather right? Does today mark the beginning of a journey that will heal my wounded heart? That scripture probably holds a clue. I'll have to read it to find out... but that isn't going to happen any time soon. After all, God and I are not on speaking terms.

———

"Okay. Time to pray." Gigi's voice calls everyone to order. Her squat frame, from which Aunt Cindy takes after, comes into view, her hands resting on her apron. With a nod from Papa, she begins, "God, our most gracious and loving Father, thank You for bringing us together again. We're so blessed by your goodness and mercy. We thank You for our family and ask that you be with Gary in Guatemala—"

"Nicaragua," Natalie corrects.

"Nicaragua. Keep him safe and help him love people with Christ's love. Let Your goodness shower the hurting people of Nicaragua, and show them Your truth."

Uncle Fred coughs. Whether it was a true cough, an after-smoke cough, or a warning for Gigi to hurry it up, Gigi moves on to the final subject of prayer.

"Thank you for this food. It is delicious and we eat it with grateful hearts."

A collective amen is drowned out by the fight for the dish of pulled pork. Over the din of battle, I hear Aunt Cindy's voice. "Mama, did you call Nina yet? She said her surgery went well."

Nina. My mother.

The words pummel into my gut. My stomach churns, heat floods my body. My arms itch, begging to be scratched. Is this a panic attack?

I need an exit strategy.

Excusing myself, the words drowned out by fresh sparring over the lone platter of corn, I head to the bathroom.

Cold water from the tap hits my face. If only I could drown out the memory of my mother. Why did Aunt Cindy have to mention Nina? Well, it's no surprise that Nina keeps important details like surgery to herself. That's the luxury of locking people out of your life—there's no one to care about you when you need help.

Why did I even come to dinner? I'm such an idiot for doing this to myself. Aunt Cindy is acting like nothing happened, as though I'm something to be ignored. She's just like her sister. I'm so stupid—

My inner dialogue is interrupted by a soft knock at the door.

"Em?"

It's Natalie. Of course. Mother Bear to the rescue.

The mirror mocks me with the image of my waterlogged face.

"Can I come in?"

Wiping a towel across my face, I give a muffled reply. "I'm fine."

"Are you?" Natalie's tone is as soft as an embrace.

Pulling open the bathroom door, I cross my arms. "I said I was fine."

Natalie strokes my arm. I shrug her away, old habits reasserting themselves.

"Aunt Cindy didn't talk about Nina just to upset us," she says.

The dirt under my nails is more interesting than what she has to say.

"She had some sort of facial surgery," Natalie continues. "Botox or something. It wasn't anything major."

"It never is." The urge to dig my fingernails into my arms is strong. Instead, I drum the fingertips of my right hand against my left arm, keeping the pressure light.

"Do you want to go somewhere and talk about this?"

I have *had it* with that maternal tone. It's time to crack the fragile ice that stands between us and the dark waters of our past.

"No, Natalie, I don't want to talk to you. I don't need *mothering*."

Natalie opens and closes her mouth like a fish.

I push past her, sighing heavily. "Sorry. Forget I said anything."

When I was a child, the striped wallpaper in this hallway invited me to race to the dining room as fast as possible. Now the stripes close in around me, like bars on a prison cell.

I am trapped.

When I get back to the dinner table and take my seat, Mark is talking about my dad's recent phone call from Nicaragua.

Natalie slips in beside him and doesn't miss a beat. "Dad said that he was riding on a bus talking with a moustached man about the price of mules. He asked the senor some questions and was deeply embarrassed to find out that it was a *senora* he was talking to!"

Everyone laughs at the anecdote, including me. My earlier tantrum makes me blush. Bashful and embarrassed, my eyes connect with Natalie. Can she see my apology? Natalie nods as if to say it's fine.

The china cabinet catches my attention. There were hours of hard work attached to that restoration. We had to strip layers of paint and sand down the edges. Neither chore appeals to me now. I *like* my layers. Rough edges define me. That's who I am. Restoration isn't necessary.

"Emma," Uncle Fred begins, "how's the old office grind?"

I take a bite of pork and swallow. It becomes stuck. Reaching for water, I shrug and hope it makes for a passable answer.

"Hey, Uncle Fred," Natalie cuts in. "Mark and I were thinking about putting in a new deck around the back. Do you think you could help us?"

Mark looks sharply at Natalie. "That's not official. I said it was a nice idea."

Natalie presses on, ignoring her husband. "We know you did a beautiful job designing the patio at your place. Maybe you would help us come up with some plans?"

Mark's jaw tightens and he stabs a piece of pork.

Everywhere I go, disaster ensues. Mark is oblivious. Natalie is trying to save me from dealing with embarrassment. She's protecting me—like a mother would. Well, no more.

"I don't work for Aunt Cindy anymore."

The noise at the table trickles off. Even Andrea looks up from her cell phone. Papa lays down his knife and fork. Jack, wide-eyed, holds his dinosaur in mid-air. Everyone's looking at me, except Aunt Cindy, who wipes her mouth with a napkin.

Uncle Fred looks from Natalie to me with a puzzled expression. "Oh."

"You quit?" Papa half-shouts from his end of the table.

Where is the rewind button when you need one?

Natalie looks at me and mouths, "Tell them."

I shake my head, but Andrea witnesses it. She puts her cell phone down. "Mom, did you fire Emma? That's so lame."

Aunt Cindy's head snaps up as slight pandemonium breaks out.

I glare at Natalie, who responds with another one of her mother-knows-best looks. That is the *last* straw.

I stand up.

"Aunt Cindy was right to fire me," I burst out. "I was a lazy employee. I've had a hard time ever since," and here I wish I could say his name out loud around my family, but I can't, "since… the wedding was cancelled."

"Wasn't that at the end of April?" Andrea whispers. Gigi's hand on her arm brings silence.

"I don't need pity jobs." Not from Aunt Cindy and not at my mother's suggestion. "And I don't need mothering." Natalie has the decency to study her plate. "And I don't need reminding that I'm not in church." No one has even brought the subject up, but they might. "I'm not in church. It's called being mad at God. I know all about it. Stop clucking at me like I'm some baby hen."

"Cluck, cluck, cluck," Jack says.

I freeze.

Papa snickers, Uncle Fred snorts, and soon everyone is laughing. Jack flaps his arms for effect. I should laugh, too, but my pride—my damn pride—makes me back away from the table. Before my feet head for the door, I know I'm leaving.

It's immature, but I don't care.

Racing down the steps and covering the distance to the car, I hop in and hope that the engine will roar to life. It does, on the first try. Slamming the car into gear, I whip out onto the street and quickly accelerate only to meet a stop sign a few hundred yards away.

Where am I going? I have no plan, no place to go. Why can't I do anything right?

Deciding to turn left, I hit the power button on the radio, hearing the melody to "Jesus, Take the Wheel" fill the car. I snap it off.

"Gimme a break. We're reuniting over a country song, Jesus? I don't think so."

Would you like to be reunited with Me, Emma?

The engine idles at yet another stop sign.

And I have no idea which way to go.

Chapter Six

Why am I so messed up? I just made a spectacle of myself at family dinner. I don't *do* spectacle anymore. That was the old me—the very old, packed in the bottom of a trunk, never to see light of day me. But all my old ways of struggling, coping, and begging for attention are coming back. I can't go down this road again.

The crunch of gravel drowns out my fears as I head to a place I haven't been in years. The dust billowing behind my tires blocks the rear view. I wish I could block out my past like that.

I stomp on the brakes. Unbuckling my seatbelt, anxious to escape the pressed atmosphere of my car, I push the door open. An echoing thud rings in my ears as I slam the door and take in the wild beauty of the river.

My feet are like deadwood, locking me in place. But I need to move. Keeping my eyes on the steady rhythm and flow of the river, I walk forward, hoping for serenity. Instead I hurtle through the air, my feet tangling with a crooked root.

A stinging sensation blooms on my knees as they scrape against the ground. I plough into the dirt like a human garden hoe. Crap. The pebbles rough up a few layers of skin, but I have no cuts. If only I did. If the rocks had sliced my skin open, I wouldn't be agonizing over this next decision.

The river stones beckon me. My fingers move expertly in search of the right sort of rock. Heavy thoughts press in on me like a storm pregnant with rain.

Suddenly, my fingers close around dark ambition.

A stone. Black, lightweight, and pointed on one end. I test the tip of the rock and know it's sharp enough to cut my hand or arm open. I would have to press hard, but it would be enough.

This rock is the key to Pandora 's Box and all the old demons that live inside it. I close my eyes, recalling the release of deep pain that comes with a cut.

"Help me," I whisper.

My cry isn't to God. It's actually to the rock I'm holding. I hope it can help ease the pain. The edges pressing into my skin feel more real than the agony of heartache.

"Remember." The memory of my grandfather's voice shoots up like a geyser. The rough side of the rock caresses my hand as it falls to the ground. *"Why does God tell His people to build altars?"*

"To remember?"

"To remember."

The pain in my hand travels up my arm and fills my body with shame. I watch the imprint of the rock fade away as the flesh rebounds. There's no blood. No cut.

I hang my head and wish for tears, but they don't come. I've reached that dark space inside me where I can no longer feel sad.

I stare at the fallen rock.

"Remember."

The word floats in my mind as the river bubbles by. What am I supposed to remember? I've spent the last two months replaying every moment I shared with Ben. I haven't spent much time thinking about God, though. Or remembering what God has done for me in the past. Is that what I'm supposed to do? Or am I supposed to recall that I am to give my pain to Him and not to any other idol?

I half-smile, thinking of the stone I was about to use. Papa would have liked the connection between stone idols and the false sense of comfort I almost pursued. But I won't be sharing this with him anytime soon.

I suddenly long for an ivory chess piece and checkered board. Only right now I feel like I'm playing against myself.

"God, help me. What am I supposed to do?"

Remember.

"How?"

Build Me an altar.

I stare at the ground, then stand up and brush my hands against my shorts. "Thanks, but no thanks, God."

I head back to the car and lock myself inside.

The silence is shattered by the repeated banging of my fist against the steering wheel. It hurts, but already I feel better. No one can say that watching UFC fight nights with Ben was for nothing. I'm able to pummel my anger straight into the steering wheel with one hit after another.

"Build You an altar? An altar? Do You know what goes on an altar, Lord? A sacrifice." I pound the wheel once more and end up blasting the horn. "There's nothing left of me to give. Do You hear me? There is no sacrifice here. I'm broken and burned up already. I'm a heap of ashes."

Give Me your ashes. I will give you beauty for ashes.

I slump against the steering wheel, the plastic digging into my shoulders. My body remembers how to feel and my eyes swell like teabags in hot water. The tears fall onto the steering wheel and then onto my legs, salty rivers that leave no stain and wash nothing away.

The growing constriction in my head pushes against my temples. Where is the Kleenex? My purse only has a Wal-Mart receipt. It will have to do.

I push open the car door once more and march to the river, the dirt flying up from my feet. I reach down and pick up as many rocks as I can hold and hurl them into the water.

"Here's Your stupid altar, God." The rocks disappear into the murky depths. It would be more fitting if the river was rushing, but it flows serenely forward, oblivious to my show of aggression. I'm like a kid throwing a tantrum while a calm parent waits for me to conclude my screaming match.

Panting, I fall back on the rocks, the dampness of the shore making itself known. The treetops impress themselves against the sky.

Me.

The hairs on the back of my neck stand up.

The beauty I offer you is the great exchange. All of you, for all of Me.

The treetops swirl effortlessly against the wind, calming me.

"You?" The thought of who Jesus is and all He's willing to give me in exchange for the spent pile of ashes I have become makes me think He's getting the raw end of the deal. "Your love?"

Could His love go that deep? Could it reach to the bottom of my barren soul and heal me? And if it did heal me, would that be enough? I thought it was enough before, but here I am, spent and broken once again.

The river flows by and I think of all the rocks under the surface, lodged in the mud, unable to move. I feel like that, unable to move forward—with my life, with my heart, and with my faith. Once again, I confirm what I already know about myself.

I am stuck.

Chapter Seven

It would be ideal if I woke up this morning with the sun dawning bright, filling my room with the promise of a new day. But it doesn't.

It can't.

I have the shades pulled down and the blankets over my head. My alarm clock's beady red eyes say it's 9:23 a.m., but it isn't until 9:44 a.m. that I convince myself to leave the coziness of my bed before my bladder explodes.

The bathroom mirror tells no lies. Last night's riverside crying session has left me with blotchy skin that looks like campfire coals and puffy eyes like marshmallows.

I also have a pounding headache. Aspirin will be a good choice for breakfast.

The blinking light on my answering machine draws me in like a well-baited hook. I press the play button before locating an aspirin, evidence of my misplaced priorities.

"Hello. This is a message for Emma Carmichael from the Lethbridge Public Library. The books you requested are here at the front desk. Thank you."

I search for a clean glass and make a plan to go to the library. It'll be the major event of my day.

Next message: "Hey Em. It's just Dad. I was praying for you tonight. I'll try and call you tomorrow. Love you."

The timestamp makes me smile. It came in around seven o'clock last night, the same time I was at the river, praying and throwing rocks. Coincidence? I think not.

Beep.

"Hi Emma. This is your cousin, Andrea." A slight pause. "Um, yeah, interesting night tonight. It kind of reminded me of the Japanese film *Exile from the Metal Moon.* Except instead of you flying away on your rocket shoes, you took off out the door. And you didn't shoot lasers out of your wrists. Anyway, you left your cell phone on the table when you rushed out. I'm leaving it with Papa and Gigi. Just thought you'd like to know."

Beep.

I wash down the aspirin with some water. What colour lasers would shoot out from my wrists if I had such a super power? At least my cell phone is somewhere safe.

The aspirin bottle is now empty. This doesn't bode well.

"Emma, it's Papa. I have your phone. Come and get it. It keeps beeping." I can hear a voice in the background telling him something. "Oh, Gigi says you should come for lunch tomorrow." My grandfather's voice becomes muffled, like he's turning away from the phone. "Are you sure? I thought we had the appointment for the oil change tomorrow."

I smile as a squabble ensues about when the appointment is for. The oil change is booked for Wednesday, but Monday requires a stop at the drugstore to fill a prescription.

"Okay, never mind all that," the message continues. "Tuesday, you come for lunch. What time? Never mind, just come. We'll see you then. Bye-bye."

Beep.

"Em, it's Dad calling again." I bet my sister talked to him last night. "I just got off the phone with Natalie... I hope you're okay. Call me when you get in."

He gives the number where he can be reached. I press my fingers against my temples. I need more aspirin.

———

I once played the role of a dung beetle in a high school play. My duties were simple. I went from my home to a fallen tree to scavenge for some dung, then double-backed. I did this constantly throughout the first act of the play while pushing a make-believe ball of manure. I was told it was symbolic of life's repetitive nature and man's desperate attempt for gain. My only line was, "I need more. I must keep going." I repeated it every time I crossed the stage.

I recite the words to myself now as I head down the aisle of the drug store. "I must keep going." My shopping cart has a squeaky wheel and feels about as useful as a ball of dung.

I find the aspirin and buy the extra-strength, extra-large bottle. Just a gut feeling I have about the month ahead.

"Emma, is that you?"

Did I mention the part in the play where my path is crossed by a hungry grackle?

"Mrs. MacDonald, what a surprise."

"I'm picking up some—"

I stare at my neighbour's bushy eyebrows and make a face void of curiosity. I don't care what kind of medicine she needs. My general observation of people is that they're a little too apt to reveal their personal health woes when you meet in a pharmacy, and these stories usually end with the need for Imodium. And that's nothing I want to know about.

"You look tired, Emma dear."

"I am." I hate being called *Emma dear.*

"And weary in spirit, too, after all that fuss at your grandparents' place last night."

The pounding in my head cranks up as I try rationalizing why she knows about that. Emulating the movements of the dung beetle, I push my cart ahead with deliberate steps. "Oh, how did you hear?"

"I read your sister's blog. She's one of my favourites. I read last week how you're in need of some employment after your aunt fired you. Such rotten luck."

My head spins like a yo-yo. "Yeah. Rotten." Kind of like dung.

"Listen, Emma dear." My grackle neighbour leans forward and touches my arm. I think she may even have yellow eyes, like the bird.

34

"I have a job for you."

She moves in closer. I can smell the potent hairspray she uses to keep her greying coif in place. Is she going to sprout a beak and gobble me whole?

"I want you to consider taking Mr. MacDonald out for a walk. It needs to be done three times a week and I just don't have the time. His constant care drains me, but I love him and can't get rid of him. We have too much history."

Mr. MacDonald is her pet schnauzer, a decrepit old dog who leaves his dung in my father's yard.

I barely nod. Even that motion makes my head throb. "Wait! You said you read about me on my sister's blog?"

"Oh, yes. And between you, me, and the painkillers, walking out of a family dinner isn't immature at all."

I'm sure she can see my tonsils for how slack my mouth feels. Her sweaty palm pats mine.

"I'm glad we had this chat. Toodles!" She struts off down an aisle, hunting and pecking for a diarrhea cure-all.

I'm a bit dazed, like a swatted fly that still has a chance to get away if it moves quick enough.

I grab two more bottles of aspirin and push my cart towards the cashier. I take a step forward, then remember that, in the play, the grackle lured me into a trap and killed me. The end of Act One found me lying on the ground, twitching.

But not today, if I can avoid it.

———

The aspirin is slow taking effect. So much for the promise of fast-acting relief. Walking into the library, the serendipity of this day is not lost on me—and I may not have one of those new-fangled smartphones, but I have a library that will give me an all-access pass to spy on my sister's blogging activities.

Signing up for the next available computer—I have to wait ten minutes—I pull open the bag of liquorice I purchased with my aspirin.

It's tough like shoe leather, making my jaws ache along with my head.

Mrs. MacDonald's words swirl behind my eyes and they're harder to digest than the liquorice. Why would my sister be writing about me on her blog? And how could she write about my temper tantrum as though it were entertainment for the masses? Didn't she know I would find out?

Well, it's probably nothing. I'm probably just overreacting because my head hurts and my neighbour's hair smelled like a latrine.

My computer seat is still warm from the person who just left. Logging on, I hold my breath, hoping Mrs. MacDonald made it all up. Maybe it was another one of her exaggerations, like the time she claimed the neighbourhood was being taken over by hoodlums because a family with five kids moved in.

A purple web banner announces that I've found "Happy Mom vs. The Laundry Pile," Natalie's blog. I scan over the chirpy description of Natalie being a stay-at-home mom and married to her best friend. According to the blog's motto, life happens while you're folding socks. How kitschy.

I search for the most recent post. It's entitled, "Why did the hen leave the dinner table?"

The colour drains from my face. Mrs. MacDonald wasn't exaggerating this time.

> I bet I win this week's Stranger Than Fiction Prize.
>
> Last night, we witnessed our own soap opera played out in my grandparents' dining room. It was quite the show.
>
> Every soap opera has its characters and this one is full of them.
>
> The loving matriarch—my grandmother, Gigi
>
> The diva—my sister, obvs.
>
> The villain—Aunt Cindy (see last week's post about Aunt Cindy firing my sister from her job. Oh yeah, I think we all see where this is heading).
>
> And since we're handing out roles, I'll just place myself as the sophisticated-who-doesn't-look-her-age supporting player. (ha!)

Natalie's blow-by-blow account paints me as a pathetic loser, nothing more than a girl void of ambition, trapped in self-pity and regret.

I read the last line: "My sister isn't a chicken, but she does have egg all over her face." Can we please stop with the clucking hen jokes?

I quickly gather my book bag, sign off the computer, and march towards the door. How could she write about me? How could she tell my life story? It's *my* story, not hers. How dare she reveal the details of my life to strangers… and weird neighbours.

Caught up in my own world, I suddenly feel a sharp stab and hear something clatter to the floor. I've knocked over a library placard. I bend down to pick it up, reading the words "Puppets and Poems, 11 a.m."

"Auntie Emma!" I feel Jack before I see him. He wraps himself around my leg, announcing, "I'm a spider monkey."

Staggering from his weight, I knock the placard over again. "Hi, Jack."

"Jack, help your Auntie Emma."

Natalie's voice flips a switch inside me and I start to shut down. The angry rant I had formulated moments ago has also decided to go the way of silence. In less than two seconds, I am mute.

"I didn't know you were going to be here." Jack is holding my hand now. "Is this the surprise, Mommy?"

"No, sweetie. But this *is* a surprise."

"Today is just full of them," I mutter.

Natalie adjusts Grace's sundress. "Why don't you sit with us for Puppets and Poems?"

"Is that today?" Jack jumps around like he's just kicked a winning goal. "Yippee! What a surprise!"

I envy my nephew's careless freedom. Natalie has violated my personal liberties and I should tell her off. Instead I choose imprisonment and find myself facing a half-hour of talking puppets who spout rhyming couplets.

"You can sit with me, Auntie Emma," Jack says, pointing to the green square of carpet in the children's section of the library.

"Sure." Anything to escape Natalie.

"No, sweetie," Natalie says. "Maybe in a little while. Auntie Emma and Mommy need to talk first."

Jack and I exchange glances. We're familiar with Natalie's demands. Jack rolls his eyes and looks as though he might object. A little girl in a red jumper is eyeing his floor mat, though, so he abandons me to claim his territory.

Natalie laughs. "Looks like you're stuck with me."

Lucky me. Biting my lip is the only thing stopping me from speaking my mind and making a scene. Wouldn't that be great fodder for Nat's blog?

Soon the presentation begins and the librarian introduces herself as Susan. She has trendy glasses and short brown hair. She holds up a puppet named Bruno the Bear and the kids giggle.

"Bruno's going to tell us about being quiet during storytime," Susan begins.

Natalie's eyes are on me. "So…? How are you after last night?"

Her mothering tone manifests like a fairy tale wolf, deceptively charming and sweet. A swift hit to the head from a puppet would change that.

"Fine," I say through clenched teeth.

"Just fine?"

"I said fine. And I mean it." I look her in the face. Curious and questioning eyes probe my own before my attention returns to the librarian and the bear.

Natalie flips her hair over her shoulders. "Fine."

Bruno the Bear is suddenly directed towards us. "Even the parents have to be quiet," the puppet says. I make brief eye contact with the librarian, who gives me a meaningful look. Bruno's paw comes to his mouth. "Shhh!"

All the kids joined in. "Shhhh."

"That's right," says the librarian in a silvery voice. "Like a special secret. Shhhh."

The librarian begins a tale about three goats and a bridge. The story is lost on me as I wonder why my sister talks to me like she's my mother, yet writes about me like I'm a joke. My stomach tightens. I can't take the stress anymore. Leaning over, I whisper, "That woman looks like my neighbour, Mrs. MacDonald."

Natalie studies the librarian. "Mrs. MacDonald is in her late sixties. That woman is barely thirty."

"You don't think she looks like Mrs. MacDonald?"

Natalie shrugs. "Not really." Her hands start clapping along with Bruno the Bear.

"Well, I think she does." I join in the clapping, but I'm off-rhythm. "Do you know what Mrs. MacDonald is up to these days?"

"Jackie, sit," Natalie says. Jack is standing up, clapping along with Bruno. He only sits down once Bruno prompts him. Natalie leans back. "Sorry, what were you saying about Mrs. MacDonald?"

"I saw her today."

"Shhh!" Bruno reminds everyone with a paw to his mouth. "Like a special secret."

The clapping dies down. Everyone in the room put their fingers to their lips. "Shhhhh."

"How was she?" Natalie asks about Mrs. MacDonald.

"Actually, she was really worried."

Natalie's eyes are fixed on Jack. "Really?"

"Yes, really."

"About what?"

"She was worried about me. It seems she read somewhere on the internet that I've been making an idiot out of myself at family dinners." I force the words out my mouth and hope they come out tough and hard.

Laughing, Natalie waves her hand. "Don't worry about Old MacDonald. She probably read my blog about last night's dinner. She's always been one to worry. Remember the hoodlum epidemic?"

Heat pours into my face. The headache makes a comeback as I find my voice. "Maybe she should be considered the soap opera's town gossip. After all, the outrageous diva role already belongs to me."

A few mothers turn and frown at us. One gestures for us to be quiet.

"Emma, you're overreacting. It was just a funny story."

"A funny story? My life is a funny story to you?"

"Blogging is just a way to sort out my thoughts. Nothing is conclusive and final on there. I'm just thinking out loud, so to speak." Natalie touches my shoulder. "You aren't acting like yourself. I'm worried about you."

"But not worried enough that your little thoughts might cause me great embarrassment, or even hurt my feelings."

Children start turning to see what the commotion is about.

Natalie opens her mouth with a ready excuse.

"Forget it," I say, standing up and pulling my bag over my shoulder. "I can't trust you, Nat. You were supposed to be a safe place for me."

The librarian coughs and waggles Bruno towards us with her hand. "Shhhh!"

I look at the puppet. "Yeah, yeah. I know." I put a finger to my mouth and then glare at Natalie. "Shhhh! Like a special secret."

Chapter Eight

The cheerful red geraniums welcome me back. I hated their happiness the first time I saw them, and I hate them even more now.

The solid oak door of the Bridgeway Home for Girls beckons me. Pulling it open ushers in the memory of the day I moved in. I was a jittery sixteen-year-old, scratching my arms, praying for my nails to cut deep enough to release my fear.

The door opens with a familiar creak. The smell of vinegar tickles my nose and I wonder which one of the girls is responsible for cleaning the entryway.

A girl with an earring in her eyebrow and a dark expression passes by. She doesn't make eye contact. I bet she's been here less than a month.

"Excuse me." My voice bounces off the walls and is absorbed by the waiting room carpet. "Is Tammy around?"

Without answering, the girl continues to walk away. I roll my eyes and pretend I was never rude like that.

It's been a while, but I know the way to Tammy's office. Taking a few steps down the hall, I take note of the girls' collages on the wall. There are angry reds and subtle blues, magazine words pasted over images of a house burning down or a little girl smiling. I study one entitled "Used to Be Seven." Seven images circle a young girl, and the words "Innocence

Lost" are scribbled in crayon. I think of the first friend I made when I was in here. Mandy. She would like this piece of art.

Thinking of Mandy reminds me of something. A rush of excitement fills my body.

I enter into the common room where the girl with the eyebrow ring is setting up a video game. I ignore her and walk over to the chessboard lying forgotten on a bookshelf.

Taking a deep breath, I slide the board out of its place. My hand brushes against the surface. It is worn and smooth. Slowly, I turn the board over and my face has trouble containing the smile that comes from somewhere deep inside me. Right where I expected to find it is an engraving: "EC 2C517." I remember burning it in with a magnifying glass. The letters and numbers glowed from the slow movements of my hands. Now, six years later, they still remain.

Emma Carmichael. 2 Corinthians 5:17: *"Therefore, if anyone is in Christ, he is a new creation; the old has gone, the new has come!"*

I wrote this the day I was baptized. It was the same day I changed my name to Emma.

Peering around the room, I calculate the odds of me escaping with the chessboard.

"Emma?"

I jump a little at the unexpected voice. "Tammy!"

"Up to your old tricks again, huh?" She gestures towards my belly, where the corner of the chessboard is showing from underneath my shirt.

———

I believe that a person's office reflects a lot about their character. Aunt Cindy has muted shades of grey and is extremely organized. Papa's study is a cozy home of good reads and comfy chairs. Tammy's office is cinnamon brown. The bulletin boards are plastered with photos and thank-you letters from girls who have lived at the Home over the past ten years. It's like sipping a cup of honey-flavoured tea.

My eyes search and find my smiling face on the board. I gulp. My wedding invitation is hanging next to a picture of Ben and me.

Tammy glances at it. "Sorry. You know I don't always get around to changing things on my board." Settling in her chair and cradling a cup of coffee, she sweeps aside her brown bangs. "What's up? Besides breaking and entering for a chessboard you vandalized six years ago."

I grin sheepishly, then sigh, collapsing on the chair opposite her. There's no use trying to pretend with Tammy.

"I thought about cutting myself last night." The words uncoil from my mouth like a snake. "I didn't self-injure. And I have no desire to do so now. I just need someone to talk to."

Tammy takes a sip of coffee. "You came to the right place. Let's talk."

Studying my bare ring finger, I gather up the courage to say his name out loud. My pulse skitters and I take a calming breath. This is a big step for me.

"It's been hard since," I swallow, "since Ben and… and everything has fallen apart. Everyone has abandoned me."

The story spills out and falls to the ground. An invisible pile forms as I tell about Ben leaving me a message to call off our wedding, and his unwillingness to return my calls and tell me why. Tammy listens patiently as I ramble on about my father's absence, my unemployment, Katie's departure, Natalie's betrayal, and how for the first time in my life I understand country music like never before. It feels like I'm in a pile up to my thighs before I finish my story.

Tamm's brow furrows. "What stopped you from cutting last night?"

Did my brain decide against it, seeing as it was a huge sanitation risk? No. The truth is much simpler. "God."

Even as I say His name, my head pounds with The Headache That Will Not Go Away. I've made it through the whole story without crying, but now tears creep up like a vine of morning glories.

Tammy waits.

"Sorry," I say, swiping at my eyes. "I'm just thinking about how mad I've been at God lately. Despite that, He's still kind to me and prevents me from making a huge mistake."

Tammy sits with her hands folded, waiting for me to continue.

"I realize it's stupid to be mad at God, but God knows me, Tammy. He knows when I rise, when I sleep, all that. So if He knows that, if He knows my past and the deep hurts that have gone with it, then why didn't he prevent Ben from breaking my heart? God knew it would go this way. He knows the future." I shift in my chair and fidget with the hem of my shirt. "Why? Why would He allow this junk to happen to me when I've already had a horrid past? The Bible says that He's promised me a hope and a future. This isn't very hopeful, you know. I've paid my dues. I've had a tough life. He owes me."

Tammy laughs. "God owes you?"

"Yeah." I smack my palm against the arm of my chair. "He owes me. I've been following His ways and doing what He's asked me to do. You know, I even prayed about dating Ben. I mean, right from the beginning. I felt like the Lord was saying yes, to go forward. And you know me, I wouldn't have opened my heart to Ben unless I knew it would be safe. So yeah, He owes me. He could have saved me this hassle if He had just said no."

"Ah." Tammy leans back in her chair. "So Jesus isn't a 'scratch my back, I'll scratch yours' kind of Person?"

"He should be."

"Then He wouldn't be just. If He was like that, you could manipulate Him to do what you want. He is God. He wants your total surrender, trust, and obedience whether life unfolds the way you want it to or not. Anyone who tells you different is lying to you, schlepping a different Jesus than the real thing."

I smile at my friend's use of the word schlepping. "The part that makes me most angry, Tammy, is that He wants me to build an altar— you know, a memorial. He wants me to mark this time in my life in some significant way."

Tammy looks at me like I've just told her I've decided to run away and join the circus.

Next, I explain to her what happened last night.

Tammy's brown eyes search mine. "You think God wants you to worship Him through all this and remember that He's good?"

"Yes."

"Even if everything is falling apart around you?"

"Pretty much."

"It makes no sense, though."

Tammy smiles and quotes scripture. "'For my thoughts are higher than your thoughts. My ways are higher than your ways.'"

"And that's it? That's the brush we use to paint over the fact that I'm in pain and He could have prevented it? 'His ways are higher'?"

"No, hon. Get your eyes off yourself. The higher way is praising Him for who He is. No matter what happens, He remains worthy of praise."

"Oh. Right." I hang my head and wish Tammy would join my pity party. But she won't. "I guess I know that."

"I know you know. And I know that you know what you need to do."

"How many times are you going to say the word *know*, Tammy?

"You know, I don't know."

I roll my eyes. Tammy is in love with her own jokes.

"You're not worried that I considered cutting myself last night?"

Tammy sways from side to side, thinking it through. "Yes and no. I'm always going to take a cut comeback seriously. In the same breath, you're here right now. That's something."

"But what if it's not enough, Tammy? I mean, what if it comes back? This urge to cut?"

"I have a plan. First, return to walking in the truth. It's a lie that cutting will help you feel better. What's the truth?"

"I can't save myself. Only Christ can redeem me. He was wounded for my transgressions and bruised for My sin. His body was punished so I don't have to punish mine."

"That's a good start. Are you ready to talk to someone about what you've been going through? A pastor, counsellor, anyone?"

I shake my head and stare out the window. "Not yet."

"Okay. Then let's move to the next best thing. Accountability and communication in a way that is safe for you right now. You remember how the daily scale works, right?"

"You ask me how I'm doing on a scale of one to ten, and I tell you where I'm at. One means I'm at risk, ten means I'm doing great."

Tammy smiles and then fusses with her smartphone. I grant her access to my safety bubble by giving her my cell number. She types it in and sets an alarm, with a reminder to text me daily. "Good girl. I always say that we train them up right." She winks at me and then grows thoughtful. "You know, Em, there's another thing to consider."

The pounding in my head lulls. "What's that?"

"You can do what I did when I felt fragile a few years after I sobered up."

"What's that?"

"I started volunteering here."

Chapter Nine

My engagement ring is currently locked in the safe in my dad's office. Dad's idea, not mine. I think he suspected I might go a little postal and throw it away. Or smelt it down in the oven along with a stranger's pet rabbit or the neighbour's dog.

The jury's out on what I should do with the ring. Return it? Keep it? Sell it? Give it away?

If my life were to flash before my eyes right now, that ring would be part of the montage. So would the memories of Ben's hand in mine, Ben's hair sticking up after a soccer match, and the way he throws his head back when he laughs.

Interesting. The only life that flashes before my eyes is Ben's, not mine. Or at least my imagined version of his life. The more I think about it, the more I come to realize that I don't know him as well as I thought I did. If I had really known him, none of this would have happened. By now, we would have been months into the honeymoon phase of our marriage.

Standing up, I look at myself in the mirror. "No time to fall apart today," I mutter. I give my reflection a faint smile. I can do this. I know I can. And it's not one of those pie-in-the-sky promises you make to yourself, like pledging to never stay up late again watching Netflix. Today is going to be different.

With a new surge of confidence, I text Tammy. I am a six out of ten.

I've been hovering around five and six for the last few days. I made it through lunch on Tuesday with my grandparents. I think they knew I was lying when I said I was good. Gigi looked hurt that I wasn't willing to share, but Papa just nodded sagely. He's a gardener. He knows all about flowers that are reluctant to open.

Gigi tried to talk about Nina and what she was up to. I asked Papa to pass the salt and then changed the subject to Mrs. MacDonald's recent diarrhea issues.

I think the lunch was a six out of ten as well

"Emma, please say you'll be my hero."

An avocado facial mask slides down my face while my cousin's voice warbles through the telephone. I figure if I'm going to turn my life around, it should start with the basics: moisturizing and manicures.

"Uh, hold on, Andrea." I dance back and forth, trying to decide if I should wipe my mask off so I can hold the phone to my ear, or just suffer the consequences and plaster the thing to my green face.

Pressing the speaker button solves my problem. I set the phone down and start waving my hands to dry my nails. "Sorry, what were you saying?"

"I'm wondering something." I hear bubblegum snap. "Could you drive me to my art class today? I'm sorry to call, but Mom said she would do it. You know how *that* goes…"

I wasn't about to malign Aunt Cindy to her own daughter. "Uh-huh, I do." I check my nails. I had ruined the finish on my ring finger when I answered the phone. "Crap!"

"Totally," Andrea says, thinking my comment was directed at her. "Anyway, Dad's out of town and I'm not talking to my best friend right now, so I can't get a ride from her. I mean, I could take the bus, but then I thought of you. I know you aren't doing anything right now—"

No need to spare my feelings.

An image of Andrea comes to mind—sitting on her kitchen counter, biting her lip and crossing her fingers, a posture of teenage hope.

"Yeah, I can do that. What time do I need to pick you up?"

"In twenty minutes."

"Twenty minutes?!" I look down at my clothes. They're leftovers from yesterday that I didn't bother to change out of when I went to sleep. My hair is in desperate need of one round of lather, rinse, repeat, and my face is still covered in guacamole.

"Well, nineteen now."

The tone of disrespect triggers an alarm bell in my mind, but I ignore it. Andrea is probably just worried about missing class.

"I'll be there in twenty-five minutes. I have a few things to do before I can leave."

"Can you hurry?" Her gum snaps again. "Okay, well, I guess that will have to do."

I'm about to reply when I hear the familiar click of the call ending.

"Thank you, Emma," I say, mimicking Andrea's voice. "You're the best cousin in the world, Emma. How can I ever thank you, Emma?"

Nothing annoys me more than ingratitude.

The avocado starts to slide down my face.

"I don't have time for this," I mutter.

Little Miss Art Class failed to mention that classes are being held on the other side of town—and it's starting in five minutes! Andrea is quite the little storyteller, too. I bet the whole tale about Aunt Cindy was cooked up. It's more likely Andrea slept in.

Should I just dump her on the side of the road? Somehow I doubt her high-sheen lips and Pokémon tanktop would deal well with the reality that comes from being stranded.

"I still can't believe Becca bailed on me, Emma. Me!" She utters a shocked gag sound. "We were supposed to go to this class together. I even talked my parents into paying for her lessons. Did I tell you that?"

All this is news to me, but I'm probably the third or fourth person to hear this tirade. It has all the signs of a story that's been told one too many times.

Caring about Andrea's personal life is positioned right between solving world peace and bikini waxing on my bucket list. I'm still annoyed that when I arrived, she said, "You're late," rather than offering to buy me a hot drink by way of thanks. I could really use a latte.

Andrea sighs. "It's so wrong, you know. We were supposed to go together."

Something about her tone suggests I'm about to see some authenticity underneath all that purple eye makeup.

"Becca was going to drive. I was going to supply the sour candies and soda pop." Andrea nibbles on her thumbnail. "We were supposed to be singing loudly to the radio and playing Chinese fire drill at four-way stops."

For a second, I see Andrea as she was six years ago—sad and confused that she couldn't play chess with Papa and me, a slight pout that things weren't going her way, but more out of melancholy than temper. I study her for a moment more. She really is hurt.

"I got ditched so Becca could work with her loser boyfriend all summer as a lifeguard."

I'm about to express some empathy when Andrea's bangle bracelets start ringing like church bells. Her hands are busy making a ponytail.

"I hope she gets a sunburn, Emma. I hope her nose burns so bad that it peels, all red and splotchy, and she looks like the inside of a grapefruit."

Cue the radio! Dr. Martha's voice comes to life as I press the dial. It doesn't take long for us to catch the gist of the conversation.

"What makes you think you're predictable and boring, Roger?" the good doctor asks.

"Roger?" Andrea says, rolling her eyes. "If that's your real name. It sounds boring and fake."

Funny, I'd been thinking the same thing.

Roger clears his throat before speaking. "Well, I was dumped by a woman who said I was predictable and boring."

"Is it true?"

"I don't know." There's an easy silence that indicates "Roger" is thinking hard about his answer. "I know that I love routine. I function best if my day has a steady rhythm to it and I know what's going to happen next."

"There's nothing wrong with that, Roger," says Dr. Martha. "Healthy people have routines they live by all the time. But let's talk about life beyond daily rituals. What about trying new things? Do you like trying new foods? Venturing out into activities you've never done before?"

This time the silence is telling. Roger is, indeed, predictable and boring. "I don't like to try new things. Not really. No."

"What are you afraid of, Roger?"

"Clowns, spray-on hair, rumours of another *Shrek* film. Other than that, not a whole lot."

"You're a bore!" Andrea announces, turning off the radio and sitting back in her seat.

"Excuse me? I was listening to that."

Andrea shrugs. "I don't know why. It's *so trivial.*"

"It is not. And anyway, the point is that I was listening to it and you turned it off—very rudely, might I add."

Andrea's feet flop onto the dashboard and the smell takes over. Day-old tuna is better than the odour now permeating my car.

"Besides," she says, tossing her bangled arm about, "Dr. Martha's only going to say he's afraid of change and that he needs to try something new. He'll have to call her back next week about the new thing he tried."

She has a point. Even Dr. Martha is a bit predictable at times.

Andrea's black toenails are leaving their imprint on my dash. "Roger is a lot like you."

"Excuse me?"

"We just passed the road to the college." Andrea points to the road we should have taken, her bracelets tinkling like chimes.

"We can take the scenic route." In a huffy silence, the car speeds ahead. My mind is full of noise and one question that asks itself over and over again. I finally give in: "How am I like Roger?"

"You're predictable."

"I am?" I can't believe I'm asking a selfish sixteen-year-old to clarify this for me.

"Yeah. Life is good for a while, you're really happy and friendly. Then life tanks and you get moody and withdrawn."

"Not true. Remember Sunday? I stormed out of dinner. That's lively and fierce. I've never done that before."

"Yes, you have."

"No, I haven't."

"Yes, you have."

"When?" I demand.

"Last March during the football game. Everyone was teasing you. Remember, we were calling you Jude the Prude because you and Ben were saving your first kiss for your wedding day? You stormed out, completely insulted."

"And rightly so." I jab my finger in the air as I say it.

"Then, at the party for Gigi and Papa, the one that was supposed to be your wedding, you dumped punch all over my mom and flounced out of the place."

"Flounced? Not possible. And I never threw punch all over your mom."

"Fine, you tripped. You still ran out embarrassed because everyone was staring at you for ruining my mother's pants."

I prepare to do a U-turn.

"That still doesn't make me like Roger. Emotional, maybe, but it's not like I'm afraid to try new things."

"Really?" A challenge gleams in Andrea's eyes.

"Really," I assert. Sticking my chin out and shaking my curls, I decide to bluff. "I'm not afraid of change or trying new things. Not at all."

"Good. Then you'll have no problem taking Becca's spot in my art class."

Chapter Ten

On the way into the college, Andrea informs me that the Mixed Media class will last six weeks. Mixed Media, it turns out, is a visual art involving paint, chalk, ink… anything, really. Right now, I'd like to camouflage myself and not draw attention to the fact that we're late.

Andrea, however, is all about making an entrance. Strutting like a supermodel, she walks over to an art table and sits next to a cute boy with hair that has been fussily designed to look like he's done nothing to it. I scramble behind her and find an open table.

I sit by myself. Surprise, surprise.

———————

Sometime later, a classmate points out the acrylic paints in the back and tells me that I'm to make up a palette. I'm not sure what a palette is. It sounds like an interpretive dance, and I'm definitely not doing that. Not in these pants anyway.

Andrea brushes past me. "You need paint. We're supposed to play with colour before the actual instruction starts. You know, get in touch with the vibe in this space."

The only vibe I'm feeling is a time-to-go premonition. I don't belong here. The clothing and hair choices of those in the room are a stark reminder that I'm not longer part of the youth of today. And what's with the ghastly eye makeup? There's a definite disco ball meets *Twilight* vibe going on. Creepy.

I need to leave. This is a mistake.

"Here you go." Andrea hands me what I can only assume is a palette of colours.

Did she have a lobotomy in the last few minutes? She just did something nice for me. Maybe I should stay, stick it out. It could be fun getting to know my cousin better.

"I actually hate these colours. I have a new vision and it doesn't involve colours from last year's fall fashion collection." She tosses her hair over her shoulder. "Enjoy."

I glance at the exit. Should I make a run for it or try the supermodel saunter out of here? If I leave now, I could probably find a decent latte and be back in time to pick up Little Miss Art Class.

Or I could leave her stranded.

The teacher interrupts my delicious plans, introducing herself as Sonya, a substitute for the regular teacher.

"Monique is finishing up an art therapy class for children recovering from trauma. They overbooked her, so I'm here to introduce you to the world," Sonya's hands trace a circle, "of Mixed Media. Monique will be back next week."

Blah, blah, blah. What was that she said about art therapy? Now that's something I could do.

I stir the colours on the palette and mix them together. The blues mix with the red, then intertwine with the rest. The green is like ivy wrapping itself around a pillar. The colours are mesmerizing.

I think I will stay.

———

"This is an interesting start, Emily." Sonya adjusts her glasses and furrows her brow. She has managed to call me Emmette, Jemma, and now Emily. Aren't artists supposed to value originality and spunk? Although, observing Sonya's choice of bright pink socks with orange sandals, maybe spunk is overrated.

"Broad strokes, Emily. Loosen up." Her hand makes a fist and jabs at the air. "Live."

I sneak a peek at Andrea. She's trying not to laugh as she copies the teacher's broad gesture and mouths the word "Live."

I scowl.

Andrea sticks out her tongue at me.

The teacher misses all of it as she adjusts her glasses again and speaks to a boy named Clarke across the room. "Clarkson, keep that colour coming. Rich tones. We want rich, rich tones."

I stare at my canvas. It holds a few streaks of grey against a stark white background. Because that's what happens when you mix all the happy colours of your palette together. They mush together into something that looks like mouldy cheese.

It's grey. All of it.

Just. Like. My. Life.

Dropping the tray to the side, I sigh with frustration.

"Frustration just means you need more patience." Papa's words come alive in my mind's eye. *"God is never frustrated. He is patient. Ask Him for patience to endure. You will miss the little things otherwise."*

Is asking for patience to endure this torturous class really a holy thing to do? Right about now, I could use a few answers, some direction, and a fruity drink with one of those little umbrellas. The only reason I'm here is because I have no life. No colour.

Sonya claps her hands to get our attention. "All right, everyone. As you know, today we are covering Mood. I know you're all anxious to begin your projects, but a refresher in the basics is essential." She spreads her hands out like a fan. "Explore the colours. Experience them. Don't just see them as colours. See them as experiences."

Is she for real?

"To encounter the depth of feeling hidden within each shade of the rainbow, you must explore the buried meaning. To do that, we're going to have a bit of fun." Sonya's arms gesticulate wildly. "I call it 'mood music.'"

I'm fairly certain my eyebrows leave my head as I raise them, all the while sending Andrea a what-did-you-get-me-into look.

Sonya presses a button on the CD player with panache.

Silence.

"Ma'am," Clarke ventures, "you just shut the machine off."

A whoosh of red fills Sonya's face as several snickers break out around the room. "Oh, this thing," she mutters.

Music pours out of the speakers: "Mr. Sun, Sun. Mr. Golden Sun, please shine down on me."

I look at Andrea to validate this moment while xylophone chimes out of the stereo. Other classmates look at each other with puzzled expressions. Just what colour are we supposed to be experiencing right now?

"Oh, for pity's sake!" Sonya looks harried as she switches the CD. She's trying to tell us about the class of eight-year-olds who were in here before us. It's hard to hear her over the laughter. Clarke even starts a rousing rendition of the childhood tune and manages to get a few people to join in. I'm close enough to Sonya that I catch her muttering. "What's the point of planning ahead when things backfire anyway?"

I know how she feels.

Mood music or no mood music, it's time to experience my grey colour. As I dump my empathy for Sonya onto the canvas, confidence takes over. A new kinship with the vibe in this place develops. I *can* understand this art thing! Maybe I am been cut out for this. Perhaps I have hidden talents that are on the cusp of emerging. My new life as an artist is before me and I'm just starting to discover my true calling. Maybe that's what it's all about.

———

Then again, maybe not.

My canvas is completely grey. Nothing else. It's a field of spores or dirty gum on the bottom of a shoe. Who can understand it? What a disappointment. I'd already imagined a killer outfit to wear to my future art show premiere.

Grabbing a sharpie from Andrea's desk, I plan a graffiti attack on my canvas.

"No more grey," I scrawl in big letters. In an attempt to be artistic, I put the exclamation point far away from the end of the sentence. There's nothing like breaking the rules!

———————

"It's rather pathetic," Andrea announces as she places the canvas in the back seat of my car.

I stare at the pen tattoo Andrea doodled on her arm. It's Japanese lettering with dark brooding eyes looking sideways. I overheard her saying it means something about a spider devouring its prey.

"You can drop me off downtown at MochaJanova's," she tells me, pulling her seatbelt on and snapping it in place. "My boyfriend is going to pick me up there once he gets off work. Can you believe lawn care takes, like, all day, and sometimes night? I, like, never see him."

Holding back a sigh, I consider my new fate as a taxi driver. I push my dark thoughts away. No more grey. No more being so down about life. I'll miss the little things otherwise.

I spy my cell phone.

Or I could miss the *silver lining* to the dark clouds. A wicked grin replaces my stoicism as I dial Aunt Cindy's number. It comes to me easily. Finally, a reason to be grateful for the million times I had to call her during my days at the magazine.

I text my plan of action while Andrea drones on about how her boyfriend works endless hours.

The country stylings of Luke Bryan keep us company as I drive downtown. My fingers pound out the rhythm on the steering wheel. The grey is starting to slide off me.

Unfortunately, it returns when I see the stormy look on Andrea's face as I pull up in front of her mother's workplace.

"Emma, what are we doing here?"

I glance up at the building I left a week ago. It looks unchanged. Somehow I'd hoped that my life being dumped upside down and emptied out like a desk drawer would leave some kind of mark.

Aunt Cindy steps out the front doors and makes eye contact with her daughter. It's a withering look, the kind that could vaporize a person.

That would solve the whole feet on the dashboard problem.

Andrea's lips twist into a snarl. Turning to me, her narrowed eyes are like lightning strikes.

"You called my mother?"

The words "Not very predictable of me, is it?" are on the tip of my tongue. As are a lot of other choice words about her conduct today. But I know she has a can of hairspray in her bag and isn't afraid to use it.

Instead, I smile. Not a smug grin, just a friendly, happy-to-help sort of smile. "Surprise!"

She huffs, bracelets clanging in a farewell song as she unbuckles the seatbelt. She mumbles something under her breath about her boyfriend, and then the slamming of the car door rattles my little car.

I take a deep breath and pray for the first time in a few days. "God, help me not to run her over as she walks in front of the car."

I shift into drive as Andrea's middle finger salutes me behind her back. I suppress the urge to jump the curb with my car and chase her on all four cylinders.

With my window rolled down, I call out, "Hey, Andrea! Thanks for inviting me. I had a lot of fun. I'll see you next week, only let's go a little earlier, okay? By the way, you owe me a latte. Bye, Aunt Cindy. Great outfit."

Not even an hour has gone by and already this art class is bringing progress into my life. I've just repaid evil with kindness. Satisfied certainty settles in my heart, then creeps up towards my brain. What have I done? I've just agreed to be in art class every Thursday with my troll of a cousin.

Chapter Eleven

The buzzer to Katie's apartment always reminds me of a giant bug hissing around my head. I'm grateful to hear it today. It means I'm granted access inside once again, and that the carton of ice cream in my hands won't melt before its time.

I practice an apology in my head: *Hi Katie, I'm sorry for the last few months. I'm a dork.* I think it's a good start.

Each step up the stairs makes me sad. Katie leaves in a few days. I could have been helping her get ready to go. Instead, I kept company with LeAnn Rimes and sang "I need you" into my hairbrush like I was auditioning for *American Idol*. A bad audition, too.

Katie's face smiles at me out the door. "I knew you would come to your senses."

I hold up the ice cream. "I come bearing gifts."

"It's not a Trojan horse is it?"

"No. It's a you-were-right-and-I-was-wrong type of gift."

Katie's right eyebrow goes up. "Celebration will depend on what kind of ice cream it is."

"Chocolate mint chip. What else?"

Katie grins like a schoolgirl. "I guess we can be friends again."

I shuffle inside and announce that I've come to help her clean up. "But first, a bowl of ice cream."

Having long since abandoned the bowls, we take turns dipping our spoons into the carton as I relive the horrors of art class.

Katie waves her spoon in the air as she talks. "I love this idea of art therapy, Em. You should take it seriously. I mean, today's piece was not a success." She looks over at the canvas I brought up from my car between my second and third bowls of ice cream. "But it's going to look great in my new apartment."

"No way. You aren't taking this with you."

"It'll be a great conversation piece when I have people over."

I push away the mental image of all sorts of new and interesting people having a great time with my best friend while I sit on my couch watching old *Gilmore Girls* DVDs.

"No way. I'm keeping it." I throw my hand in the air like Sonya did earlier. "It speaks to my soul."

"Suit yourself," Katie says, scraping the bottom of the carton. "You know what I think? I think Andrea is going to be a good person to have around."

"What? Did you not hear the part about her calling me predictable and using it against me?"

"I did. But seeing as you won't be spending much time with Natalie, Andrea's a good option."

"How do you know I'm not spending time with Natalie?"

"I read it on her blog." Katie inspects the carton for any remaining bits. "Oh yeah, she has her readers betting on how many days you won't talk to her for."

I can feel the beginnings of a mammoth headache creeping in. "What?"

"Mmmhmm. I put my bet down as ten days. Can you hold out that long? I could get a subscription to *Crafting Monthly* if I win."

"What?" Rising from my chair, I stalk over to the sink. "You're kidding, right? My sister wouldn't do this to me."

Katie dries her hands off on a tea towel and starts laughing. "Calm down, Emma. I'm kidding. Well, I'm just kidding about the bet thing. She did mention on her blog that you and she weren't talking."

I grab the tea towel from her and snap it at her head. "Why would you kid about something like that?"

"Because I won't get to see you freak out like this once I'm gone.

60

And speaking of making you freak out, you'll never guess what I found when I was cleaning out my stuff."

"Your *Dancing with the Stars* sweatshirt?"

"Nope. I think that's still at my parents' house." Katie rummages through her purse and holds up a DVD case. "Tada!"

"What's that?"

"The video of your engagement party."

———

"I'm not watching it."

A half-hour later, Katie is shaking a bag of microwave popcorn into a bowl. "You're going to watch it, Em. *We're* going to watch it."

"No. Remember what happened last time? I was a mess of mascara and snot. I drank half a bottle of Pepto-Bismol in the first five minutes. That's why I had you hold onto it for me. I'm not watching it."

Katie takes a handful of popcorn. "Suit yourself."

"Hey! Wait until we're seated." I grab my own handful, but remain standing.

"I thought you weren't going to watch it with me?"

"I think we can find a Johnny Depp flick somewhere in your collection. We'll watch that instead."

"No."

"No?" My voice is as soft as a puppy's whimper. I sit down.

Katie walks over to the DVD player and inserts the disc. She hits play. I prepare to heave over the side of the couch.

The screen starts out black, then comes to life with music and a blue page that says "Emma and Ben: The Beginning of Forever."

Oh puke, who thought of that title?

My stomach is knotted like a well-tied shoelace. I can't go through with this. Is that my pulse racing or shortness of breath? My upper lip sweats profusely. I think I'm about to have an anxiety attack.

Ben and I watched this video together once, only I hadn't paid much attention at the time. Ben had his arm around me. My head was on his shoulder and I kept thinking about what it would be like when we were married and we could say goodnight rather than goodbye at the end of an evening.

"I can't do this." I stand up, only to have Katie grip my arm.

"Yes, you can."

It's Katie's tone. She has a way of saying something in such a way that you just have to do what she says. I've seen her use it with dogs before.

Photos fade onto the screen. Ben and I looking out from behind a tree. Ben giving me a daisy, then tucking it behind my ear. Another intimate portrait of us looking at each other, almost nose to nose. This last photo is full of emotion. I can almost feel Ben's breath on my face and the way my lips had twitched wondering what it would feel like to be kissed by him.

The scene opens up to me standing in front of the fireplace mantle at Gigi and Papa's place.

"Emma!" Katie shouts. "You look amazing here. How did you get your hair to look so great?"

I punch Katie in the arm. "Some strange girl I know styled it for me."

"Well, that girl is a miracle worker. I think you should give her a car."

"I should dump popcorn on her head."

I let out a breath and relax a little. Katie is doing her best to make this easy for me. It's thoughtful, but it's like a barking dog competing with your doorbell to let you know someone has arrived. My head hurts from the clashing noise of the DVD and my thoughts.

Dad's voice begins with a preamble of the event. Scanning the room, he points out all the little decorations Natalie and Gigi put up around the living room. My friend Mandy walks by in a zebra print dress, saying, "It's time to party-hearty!"

"Mandy, you're such a goof!" my voice sounds, off-screen. The camera quickly pans back to me and zooms in. My image is blurry, then snaps into focus.

"Here is the bride-to-be!" Mandy's voice pronounces.

Starting to choke on my popcorn, I croak, "Pause it."

Katie hits the pause button. "Do you need some water? Are you okay?"

I wave towards the screen. "Look at me, Katie. Look at me. I'm radiant. Look at how happy I am. I'm glowing like Roma Downey being sent from heaven with a message."

Katie looks at the screen, then back at me. She is silent.

"I miss her," I say, walking towards the screen. I kneel down and touch the TV, fully aware of how silly I look. "I miss that version of me. She's so sure, confident, alive."

Katie stuffs a handful of popcorn in her mouth. "Maybe you should shower more often."

"Shut it, Katie." I turn my attention back to the TV and release the frozen version of myself by hitting play.

Through the TV, my face shines with happiness. I wish I could whisper in her ear and warn her what's to come. "You have no idea what's in store for you, Emma Carmichael. You have no clue how the light is going to be snuffed out of your eyes."

The camera suddenly pans over and I suck in my breath.

Ben.

Gorgeous, make-my-heart-pound, amazing Ben.

"Boo!" Katie yells, throwing popcorn kernels at the screen. "Boo to the jerk who broke my best friend's heart."

I am unable to tear my eyes away from the screen. It's like watching a car accident in slow motion. It's too awful not to watch.

There's Ben. He's looking at me in the video. He loves me. It's all over his face.

My heart stops. The combined anxiety of the past nine weeks has found its way to my stomach and I'm about to be sick.

He looks wonderful and in love.

And now we're apart.

"Are you okay?" Katie asks.

I shake my head and continue to analyze his face. Why didn't I pay more attention to those criminal shows where they scrutinize people's faces to know if they're lying or telling the truth? Is that a flare of the nostrils? Wait, was that a twitch of the eye? Does it mean he's having doubts? That he's putting on a big show? That he has indigestion from the spinach dip?

"Maybe I can't do this." I grab at the popcorn for something to do.

"You can and you will," Katie said. "It's time."

Dad zooms the camera to a closer shot of Ben. He's wearing the striped polo shirt we went shopping for together. He tried on four shirts before choosing this one, but we both knew the shopping trip was just a veiled excuse to hang out together.

"Well, what do you say, Ben, about today?" Dad asks.

"Today? What? Oh, is something happening today?" His dark eyebrows travel up in that familiar way and his eyes are full of mirth. "Hey Emma, is something important happening today?"

The camera pans over to me as I play along. I put a playful finger to my chin and tilt my head to one side. "Hmmm… something important? Huh. I can't think of anything." I shrug and smile flirtatiously.

Gosh, I miss that. I miss feeling like a woman. Somehow Ben's love made me feel like I was a woman. Conversely, his discarding of me made me feel like a little girl again. Like a scraggly, hair-falling-out-of-my-braids little girl.

"Oh, wait." Ben's fingers snap and I look up from my reverie. His voice is like honey melting into my soul. "I just remembered something."

On the DVD, he sidles up closer to me. "Really. What is it?" My eyes dance. I'm glowing like a candle in a window.

When Ben grabs my hands in the video, I look away, crushing popcorn in my hands in an attempt to erase the memory of his touch. My chest is tight and I go through a mental checklist of heart attack symptoms.

Now it's my turn to throw popcorn at the screen. "Boo! Don't listen to him, Emma."

I jump in surprise as Katie joins in. We're soon yelling loud enough that I miss what Ben says. It doesn't matter. The Emma on the screen has heard it. I watch as my old self is pulled into a hug. Ben looks straight at the camera and winks.

I grab both sides of the popcorn bowl and punch it forward. Ben's smiling face is covered by a white blizzard of popcorn.

And suddenly, I find my voice: "Boo to you, Ben! Boo to your cute polo shirt and nice eyes. Boo to your perfect teeth and strong shoulders and great hugs. Boo to you, Emma! Boo to your happy smile and your white dress and… and…" I look at Katie for help. I'm running out of steam. "…and boo to your great hair!"

Katie looks at me solemnly. Is she going to celebrate that I finally let out some of my feelings or is she going to chide me for wasting all the popcorn?

"Emma," she finally says with great seriousness. "Never 'boo' great hair."

I stare at her for a moment before cracking up. Katie's smile goes wide as she joins me. "You're right, O wise one. Forgive me."

We burst out laughing. It's just like old times, when our weekends were rife with laughter, writing college papers, and trying to decipher men's behaviour.

It feels so utterly normal.

Chapter Twelve

The ceiling in my room has a patchy paint job. I noticed it the first morning I woke up here. It reminds me of what my life is like: I'm a mess. I need a change of perspective. Maybe a plan of action. And quite possibly an IV drip of espresso to get me moving.

Sitting up in bed, I survey my room. Strewn clothing is everywhere, along with books, and magazines. Notes and cards are tucked in drawers haphazardly. Is that a nacho plate in the corner? Ugh! When did I become such a pig?

I *am* avoiding life. I've become one of those people you see on TV who's in complete denial that they need to move on. I'm two steps away from having a pair of cats and eating whipped cream out of a can.

I look at my hair in the mirror. Dear God, I'm not going down like this. Not with this hairdo. I have to do something. My life needs a jumpstart.

Spying my iPod on the floor, I plug it into the stereo. I scroll through to find some music and deliberate between High Valley and Brad Paisley. Forget it. I'll just stick to the classics: Reba McEntire, "Starting Over Again."

Several hours later, my final act of bedroom cleaning is to affix a note over the bad paint job on the ceiling. On it, I write the first scripture I ever memorized when I was at the Girls Home:

He who was seated on the throne said, "I am making everything new!" Then he said, "Write this down, for these words are trustworthy and true." (Revelation 21:5)

It was easy to memorize because it was short and to the point. And if I'm honest, I memorized it because it reminded me of cutting. When I cut, I would scar and then heal. My skin became new again, fresh and ready to take another hit so my heart wouldn't have to. Slowly, over the course of time, I came to believe that it was God who made all things new, not me or my flesh. The scripture became a lifeline. I'm hoping it will once again be up to its saving status. I could use some *new* in my life.

Only, when God makes all things new, He usually makes the old things new. He restores them. I was kind of hoping for something original, like a flashy handbag from the Shopping Channel.

The cabinet in my grandparents' house was old and then restored. Papa reminded me of that when he gave me the rock with the scripture notation.

The message on the ceiling will serve to remind me that Jesus is making everything new. Whether I like it or not, Jesus is working towards that end. I could cooperate and make the process easier.

Punching the pillow seems like a good way to let out my frustration. It's no use. I can't run from everything. I can't avoid life—or—God forever.

Well, at least my room is clean. Cleaning it didn't hurt; it just took time and a good soundtrack. Do I really want my heart to continue to be a messy place?

"God, I'm not ready to surrender to You. Please make me willing. Please help me to let go of fear and trust You."

I give the pillow one last punch.

———

"Layers."

The word hangs in the air, thick and full. Andrea and I are late for art class once again. At least this time I have a latte in hand as I slide into my seat.

"Today's exercise is all about building layers in your work," Monique, the new teacher, beings. "I want to see rich dimensions. Multi-dimensions. We're going to use the media we have available to us. Newsprint, paper, plastic bags, fabric, and anything else you deem necessary. Perhaps a receipt in your pocket will inspire you."

My eyes wander as she talks about the different uses of glue and acrylic paint. Most of the people in this class are teenagers. With eager eyes, they drink in Monique's words as though they're shots of Red Bull.

I feel inept. What am I doing here?

"The goal of this course is to create art using all sorts of media and materials. In our final class, you'll present a piece of work that you created using the four elements we've chosen to focus on: mood, layers, colour, and theme. You'll begin your pieces on the fifth week, and on the sixth week you'll present them."

The door to the classroom is only ten feet away. Perhaps I could escape out of it and just wander the halls. Then, when class is over, I could wring Andrea's neck. Just for fun.

"One aspect of my job is teaching art therapy to people who have undergone trauma."

I face forward, new hunger filling my eyes.

"Sometimes people encounter a situation that's painful and they don't have words for it. They can, however, find a colour or magazine picture that represents some aspect of their experience. As human beings, we encounter many emotions in various experiences. These emotions are layers. They add substance and texture to reality.

"I won't use the onion analogy, because it's trite. Yes, onions have layers, but what's the purpose of peeling an onion of all its layers only to find more onion? The layers I'm referring to represent different things. I want you to think of the earth. Think of how the earth has soil on top. When you start to dig through silt and sediment, you reach bedrock. Then you need new tools, new skills to dig further and unearth precious gemstones.

"In essence, that's what you're creating with the use of layers. Consider the blank canvas to be the soil. Each layer you add to your work becomes part of the dig. It becomes one layer closer to the gem. The precious jewel is the final layer, what the eye sees first. It's your work of art. You're giving the world a view they don't normally see. That can only be created through layers."

A minute later, class members disperse to various corners of the room, looking at the materials available to them. Paint chips, newspaper, wallpaper swatches, and yarn are divvied up. A voice rising above the din informs me that there are several types of Mod Podge, glue, and paint available for use.

"You don't seem anxious to start," Monique says, approaching my table as everyone else gets to work. Her trendy frames bring out the blue in her eyes.

"I don't even know what I'm doing here." I give a quick explanation of my cousin's impromptu invite to class. "I'm not talented in any artistic way. Last week was a disaster. I thought I could express my feelings about…"

Monique's pencilled eyebrows go up in question, waiting for me to finish.

"Never mind." I'm not going to tell a complete stranger about Ben discarding me like roadkill. I'd rather keep that buried.

Buried.

Layered.

How about that? Maybe I do have something to contribute to this class.

The teacher clasps her hands. "I saw a spark of something just now. You look inspired."

Tilting my head, I consider my canvas. "I don't know yet. I just have an idea."

"Ideas are what start change."

Walking towards the burlap, I hope that will be the case.

––––––––––

"Then I used my nail polish to cover up the anime drawing underneath," Andrea says in the car on the way home. "After that, I took a knitting needle and dipped it in nail polish remover and etched in details to create my newest manga character for an anime film script I'm writing. I call her Stressa." She points to the neon green halo around the intense-looking character. "She's a lifeguard to her people who live in the sea."

"Hey, maybe you can give that to your friend Becca," I say, keeping my eyes on the road. "She's a lifeguard, right? You can show her that there are no hard feelings over quitting art class."

I am *so* good at this older, wiser cousin stuff.

Andrea brushes her bangs out her eyes. "Stressa inhales some potent chemicals that are dumped in the water by some big money corporation and goes mental. She mortally wounds her best friend in order to save the man who dumps the toxic waste into their home. Wouldn't Becca appreciate the poetry of this piece?"

"Right."

I'm *so* over my head with this older, wiser cousin stuff.

"Maybe you should send your piece to Ben."

I look at Andrea out of the corner of my eye. "He wouldn't appreciate the poetry of the piece," I retort.

I think back to my own creation, the one sitting in the back seat. I cut the word "me" out of a magazine and then glued burlap over it. I followed it with two swatches of wallpaper and a wide strip of plastic wrap. Then I let Andrea draw a word bubble on it. The result was a large, hillish mound of textiles with the words "Let me out!" scrawled on the canvas.

Someone came by when I was returning the glue and wrote "Cocoon" on it. Monique saw it and held it up to the class as an example of getting in touch with one's inner soul, and examining the walls we build around ourselves.

The truth is that I grabbed the last three items on the supply table. I cut out the word "me" because the person next to me said, "Here, use this." After that, I just covered it all up using glue.

There isn't any poetry in my piece. And as for showing Ben… well, I haven't been able to get a hold of him. If I did find him, my first words wouldn't be, "Hey, look who's the new Matisse!"

What would I say to Ben if I saw him again? My mind would probably go as blank as a canvas.

"Did you read your sister's blog today?"

I glance at Andrea, who's studying her smart phone.

"Uh, no. Why? What does it say?"

"She wrote about how little Jack bathed the cat in the toilet last night."

My heart squeezes tight as I think about Jack and baby Grace. Being mad at Natalie has cut me off from my niece and nephew. I don't like that.

Andrea reads the post out loud and we laugh together. Only Jack would think of using bubble bath in a toilet. The cat survived, and so did my sister.

She normally would have called me to tell me about something like that. I'm trying to remember why we're not talking…

"This next blog post is about your mother."

Oh, right. That's why—Natalie and her ability to blab about my life to the whole world.

"She says here that your mother is…" She trails off. "…cold and hard like a frozen block of butter. Hey, is that true?"

Clearly, Andrea has never spent time with her mom's sister. If she had, this question would be a no-brainer.

"Nina isn't what you would call a warm personality," I say.

"Nina? Why don't you call her Mom?"

I pull up to an intersection and wait to turn left. I pretend that I'm concentrating on the traffic. It's ruse, though. There is no traffic.

Turning down the street I used to drive to get to work, a sense of nostalgia overwhelms me. The going-to-work feeling grabs at me and I suddenly wish I had a job to go to.

I pull up to the curb next to the magazine office and hope Andrea will jump out and take her questions with her.

"Why don't you call her Mom?" Andrea repeats.

My cousin never does what I want her to do.

"It's complicated."

Andrea shrugs. "Try me."

"Okay." I breathe out. "Nina has a lot of goals, and being involved in my life isn't one of them. Plus, she asked me never to call her 'Mother' or 'Mom' in public, as it ruins the image she's trying to portray. Apparently it makes her feel old. Plus, a mom is someone who's there for you. Someone who takes care of you and shows up when you need her. She chooses to be there for you over everything else that's happening in her life because she knows it's what you need. Love. Support. Encouragement. Those words aren't in Nina's vocabulary."

Andrea studies her fingernails. She's bored with our conversation. Typical.

A knock on my window makes me jump. It's Aunt Cindy, her tired face in a tight scowl. "Are you coming? I'm not going to wait all day."

Andrea unbuckles her seatbelt and opens the door. "Sure thing, Cindy. Sorry to have kept you waiting."

Did she just call her mom by her first name?

"Don't get smart, Andrea."

"Sorry, Cindy." Andrea slams the door.

I cringe. I need to remind her about slamming doors. I unroll my window to tell her, but instead Aunt Cindy asks, "Why are you calling me by my first name?"

"Because," Andrea says, glancing back. "You have to earn the title of Mom. Until then, you're just Cindy to me."

My mouth drops open. Oh no! What can of worms did I just open?

Chapter Thirteen

"Happy Canada Day!" I walk into the empty patio area at the Bridgeway Home for Girls.

Tammy places a lawn chair down and then greets me with a hug. "I thought your text said you had other plans for today."

I shrug. "I do. I just thought I could come early and help you set up for the Family Cookout. It requires a bit of muscle power to pull it off, if I remember correctly. Put me to work."

Tammy pinches my bicep. "Okay, Muscles. You can set up the lawn chairs in clusters of two or three. And try and put them in shaded areas. Some of the girls' grandparents are coming and we want to keep them comfortable."

Unfolding the chairs, I find myself missing my dad. He was the only one who came to see me at the Canada Day cookout when I was here six years ago. We hadn't known how to talk to each other, so we just sat side by side watching a family play Frisbee.

Who will sit in these chairs today?

The patio fills up quickly as all the girls and staff come out to put up decorations, food, and seating for everyone. The air is mixed with chatter and someone has put on a Greg Sczebel CD to get everyone in an upbeat mood.

Sweat runs down my back by the time one of the girls and I manage to finish tying balloons to the back of the chairs. We high-five when the last cluster of red and white balloons is secure.

I'm finally left alone to survey our hard work.

Tammy approaches me with a glass of water. "You look thirsty."

"Thanks."

"No, thank you, Emma. You didn't have to help today."

"I know. I wanted to." The light breeze feels refreshing against my skin.

"I've enjoyed reading your texts over the past week and a half." Tammy scans the area, making sure everything is ready. "Almost every day has been at least a seven or higher for you."

"Weird, isn't it? I don't have any desire to cut myself at all. But the day before I came to see you, it really seemed like a possibility. Am I crazy?"

Tammy yells out some instruction to a staff member before responding. "No, you aren't crazy. Extreme stress brings out our old ways of solving problems. It's normal to think about how you used to cope. If you aren't handling stress properly, you'll look for a way to escape reality. Some people escape through movies or books, others use alcohol, drugs, whatever. It's all false comfort."

I cross my arms.

Tammy touches my shoulder. "Em, it's not wrong that your heart needs comforting. You know that, right? It's only sin when you seek comfort apart from Christ."

That's too heavy a concept for me right now. I change the subject. "I'm in an art class."

She studies my face, then reaches for my empty glass. "Look who's holding out on me! That's great, Emma. See, you've given yourself permission to move on. Moving on isn't as bad as you think."

I shrug and stare at the lawn chairs I set out earlier.

I may have given myself permission, but Tammy has no idea how hard moving forward is when you're stuck.

———

"Breathe it in, Emma. It's a fresh start." Katie takes a deep breath and then sticks her hand out the window and wiggles her fingers.

This stretch of N
and I will take for a w
and then Katie and I v
she'll load up her aunt's

I can feel our time r.

The green mountain.
over them, heavy with imr.

"It's breathtaking," I say

"Yeah, it is." Katie's eye.
reach her aunt's place before i
crossed the border. She can b
she's not behind the wheel.

My secret wish is to pull
watching the wildflowers paint
Katie where she needs to be.

...g around
...st the hills won't get

"Massachusetts!" Katie calls out.

I add the state to the list of license plates we've seen since we started the drive. "That makes eight states in total."

Katie squints at the sky. "I hope it doesn't rain. We aren't far from Aunt Thuy's place. Probably an hour or so."

Settling into silence, I let the beauty of nature keep me company. It makes me think of Psalm 19. I dig around in my backpack and pull out the Bible I had packed reluctantly.

The heavens declare the glory of God; the skies proclaim the work of his hands. Day after day they pour forth speech; night after night they reveal knowledge. They have no speech, they use no words; no sound is heard from them. Yet their voice goes out into all the earth, their words to the ends of the world.

It's true. Nature has a way of turning my eyes back to God, reminding me of how much I need Him. I'm small like the Brown-eyed Susan, a flower that would bloom for a season on the valley floor only to wither and die while the mountains stand strong through years of rain and snow.

ere?" I whisper in my heart. "Would

and significant way on this trip? Not with

s just meet together so I can encounter You.

nt love for you."

amen, I stare out the window.

urns on the radio and fiddles with the buttons. We high

he voice of our favourite advice guru comes through loud and

ar.

"I'm Dr. Martha Hunt. With me on the line is Juanita from Arizona. Hi Juanita."

"Hey Dr. Martha. How are you doing?"

"Just fine. How can I help you?"

"I need some help with James. He's listless, he won't eat, he won't get off the couch and go for a walk with me. I am at my wit's end."

"He sounds quite sad. Has there been any major changes to his life lately?"

"Well, his best friend Mabel was hit by a car last week."

Katie gasps. "How awful!"

Juanita continues, "He just mopes around the house. He's not even interested in my slippers anymore." She chokes back a sob. "He's the only dog I have. I can't lose him. Help me, Dr. Martha!"

Katie bursts out laughing, then turns down the radio. "What is it with people treating their pets like they're real people? It's unreal!"

"I know. Take my neighbour, Mrs. MacDonald. That dog of hers is treated like a pampered baby. You won't believe what she wants me to do when I walk Mr. MacDonald."

Katie whips her head to look at me. "Did you just say that you're walking that demon dog of your neighbour's?"

"Yep. But that's not the worst part. She wants me to dress him in his walking shorts for the summer. And then take them off when we get back home so as not to," I use air quotes to emphasize the ridiculous, "allow the sweat to permeate his fur."

Katie grunts. "I hope you're making good money."

"If I get a dollar for every time the dog stops to do his business, I'll be a wealthy woman."

76

Apparently, Mrs. MacDonald isn't the only one who has diarrhea issues.

Dr. Martha entertains us for another forty minutes. Who knew there were so many people with pet psychiatry problems, teenage body issues, and sock fetishes?

An hour later, I realize we haven't said a word since Dr. Martha signed off. What a waste of our precious remaining time together!

"Congratulations, Emma," Katie finally says, as though sensing my thoughts. "You've gone a full four hours without mentioning Ben's name."

"Only because I haven't said anything at all," I point out, opening a bag of red liquorice. I offer Katie a piece.

Between bites, she says, "It's still a win in my book. It means you've made it this far without pining for him."

"I'm a silent griever." I take a hard bite out of my liquorice.

"But you haven't been grieving. You're not even moping. You're just quiet. Pensive, maybe. But in a good way."

Katie's wrong. I may not be talking about him, but that doesn't mean my mind isn't playing a movie montage of our time together. Nothing is safe, but she doesn't know that. Everything is somehow connected to a Ben memory. I stare at the blue floor mat. He once helped me wash the car and insisted we hose down the mats. Then he sprayed me with water and I squealed.

Katie needs to know that I'm going to be okay before she leaves, though. I shrug and say, "It's the new me. Quiet, thoughtful and—"

"—holding out for country superstar Blake Shelton to write a song about you."

"It could happen."

"Right, and Kim Kardashian is going to be the next Meryl Streep."

I roll my eyes, refusing to even dignify that with a response. The truth is, I'm going to miss this.

Chapter Fourteen

"Brace yourself for impact." Katie is serious as we walk up the porch stairs. "My aunt is different from the members of my family you've met, Emma. She's as Vietnamese as the rest of us, though. She's loving and sweet, but Aunt Thuy won't cushion her words. Don't get offended."

I note the ferns in the shaded flowerbed. "Katie, anyone whose name sounds like a bird call is going to be harmless."

Katie's left eyebrow quirks as she rings the doorbell. "Okay, but don't say I didn't warn you."

A floral porch swings begs for me to sit down and take in the view of the mountains, but the door quickly opens, revealing a petite woman who doesn't look like she's in her fifties. Her black hair is sweetly curled in at chin length, complimenting her broad lips. I don't see anything odd about Aunt Thuy, except maybe her shirt, which says "Prince Harry is my Prince Charming" in bold letters.

"Ma nam." Katie nods her head at Aunt Thuy in greeting.

"Cho con!" Aunt Thuy says, welcoming Katie in the traditional greeting. She ushers us into the house.

"Ma nam, do you remember my best friend Emma? You met her at our graduation last year."

Aunt Thuy's eyes squint in scrutiny. She looks me up and down, then a smile appears, confirming that I have passed inspection. "Yes, Emma. You look good. So nice to see colour in those cheeks."

See, what a sweet bird. She's chirping love my way.

My stomach growls as I set my bag down. The food smells so good; I'm afraid that if I inhale, the calories will go straight to my thighs.

Aunt Thuy points out the living room and the hallway to our bedrooms.

The moment she's out of earshot, I grab Katie's arm. "Why is Prince William here?" I whisper, reaching out to touch the life-sized cardboard cutout staring at us from between the sofa and a row of potted plants.

As though hearing me, Aunt Thuy's voice barks like a sergeant, "Don't touch the future king."

I yank my hand back. "Sorry." Then, making eyes at Prince William, I add, "Your majesty."

Aunt Thuy hustles out of the room and I look to Katie for explanation.

"I guess I'm not surprised," Katie says. "Aunt Thuy must be going through a phase."

"You mean there's been other stages."

"Oh yes. She jumps from one obsession to the next. I've always thought she was a bit ADHD. She'll learn everything she can about a random topic and then move on. Trust me, don't play Jeopardy against her. You'll just embarrass yourself." Katie points to the wall full of photos. "The British royals aren't the first people to get the full Aunt Thuy treatment."

I squint to inspect one of the pictures, framed and mounted prominently in the middle of the wall.

My eyes go wide. "Is that your aunt and Justin Bieber?"

"Aunt Thuy went nuts for the Biebs. She got detained by mall security once for mowing down a gaggle of preteens just to get close to him."

Aunt Thuy marches in. "Those guards tried to remove me from the crowd. I started singing 'Never Say Never' and they let me go."

"I thought they threw you out," Katie says.

"Katie, I keep telling you, you can't believe everything that shows up on YouTube." Aunt Thuy smiles at me. "That's old news, anyhow. Justin came into my life right after I ran out of original *Dr. Who* episodes to watch on DVD. His music got me through. But now," she claps her hands, "now, I'm all about Wills and Kate. See?"

Katie and I look at a photo of the Duke and Duchess waving to the crowds during a recent trip to the U.S.

"Do you see me there in the photo?" Aunt Thuy asks.

Katie and I both lean closer.

"I'm next to the woman wearing the pink fascinator that's shaped to look like a flamingo."

"Found you!" Katie points to a short woman wearing a lime green shirt that reads, "I'm Holding Out for Harry."

Katie's warning is starting to make sense now.

Katie rolls her eyes and follows her aunt to the kitchen. "Ma Nam, did you make Pho?"

Aunt Thuy nods her head proudly with her hands folded in front of her waist. "I did. Last time I made this, everyone loved it. My friends and I had just gotten together to discuss *The Hobbit*. Which reminds me, Katie, I have some slippers for you. They're fuzzy versions of Bilbo's feet. You'll love them. Anyway, they begged me to make more—my friends, not the slippers." She gestures at the arrangement of meat, broth, and noodles on the table. "As for all this, well, I don't know. I was in such a hurry! Maybe I didn't let the broth sit long enough. You'll have to taste it and tell me."

Once grace is said, Katie instructs me on how to assemble my meal. She points out how to mix in the mint leaves and the bean sprouts. As I take the first bite, I want to sing the Hallelujah Chorus. The food is glorious.

"Last time I saw you, Emma, you were with that handsome young man. Rumours were whispered that you were on track to become engaged. So?"

I slurp a noodle and change my mind about Aunt Thuy. She's a bird of prey.

Katie jumps in to answer for me. "Ma nam, why don't you tell Katie about the time you met Mel Gibson?"

"Oh, it was nothing. All that social media business hadn't caught on yet, so the tabloids never found out. And it needs to stay that way. At least, that's what I agreed to with Mr. Gibson's lawyers." Aunt Thuy looks at me with intense expectation. "If I didn't know better, I'd say my niece was trying to change the subject. Has your young man found a job yet? You would think that after four years of school the process would be easier for him."

Katie flushes with embarrassment before gamely trying a second diversion. "Oh, I forgot to tell you, ma nam. Cousin Hoa said that she wants to take us shopping when we get to Toronto."

I reach for the water pitcher and refill my glass, hoping the change of subject sticks this time. "Shopping? Yes, you of all people need more clothes, Katie."

Aunt Thuy stirs her broth while looking at me. I can't help but think of a hawk circling its intended victim. "I notice you aren't wearing an engagement ring," she says. "I know when something's amiss. What's going on?"

I stare at my left hand and feel naked.

"Ma nam," Katie says quietly, "they aren't together anymore."

"I am so relieved to hear that." Aunt Thuy's countenance brightens. "He didn't seem like the kind of man who could get a good job. You could tell he spent more time with his hair than with his books."

Katie looks like she's about to spit out her soup. "Yeah, he was in love with his hair."

"I like his hair," I say softly.

"You sound pathetic, Emma," Aunt Thuy says. "You sound just like me the time I found out Pluto was no longer considered a planet. Tell me you've accepted this."

Katie and I exchange a glance. How can I accept something that has brought a decline in my health, self-esteem, and fashion choices?

"Well, you just have to move forward," Aunt Thuy continues. "You can't stay still. It's like I learned during my stint as a line-dancing instructor. If you don't move, you'll be pushed over and get a cowboy boot to the head."

I slurp my broth. Katie is focused on refilling her glass. No help whatsoever.

"Yes." Aunt Thuy's determination is clear as she slaps the table with vigour. "And I know exactly how you are going to do it, Emma."

"How do you propose that?"

Aunt Thuy crunches down on a tightly wrapped spring roll. "Oh, it's a surprise."

————

Bungee jumping, bull riding, and even geocaching would have been better ways to move on than this surprise. Instead Aunt Thuy takes us to a church service at a Bible Camp just down the road. I walk into the sanctuary only to be greeted by large lettering that declares, "Never Let Your Memories Be Bigger Than Your Dreams." The banner hangs above the platform.

The words have me rooted to the spot. Katie and Aunt Thuy shuffle into a row, but my eyes are glued to the sign. I finally wiggle into my seat, feeling jumpy. Why am I so anxious?

I jerk forward as something hits my arm. A mother and daughter pass by. The young girl's backpack is inches from my arm. The mother notices me wince and apologizes for her daughter. She then looks at the young girl and says, "Why did you bring that old bag with you? I told you to leave it in the car."

The daughter crosses her arms sullenly. "I need it, okay?"

Watching the interchange, my mind pulls me towards memories of my own mother. I try to shake it off. I learned long ago that in order to stay healthy and strong in my search for emotional stability, it's best to put my mother in another room of my heart and shut the door.

I study the girl in front of me, looking at her bulky sweatshirt. The sleeve-ends are wrapped around her thumbs. I feel a familiar tug but can't put my finger on what it is. Are my dreams trying to surface?

For now, I just count it a blessing to get up each day and make it to nightfall without crying. I've gone two days without crying. One more day and I'll be able to wear mascara with confidence. That's my only goal right now.

I obviously need some new dreams. If I'm honest with myself, truly honest, I'd say I want Ben back. I'm not ready to let him go.

New dreams mean admitting things about yourself. Hard things.

A man named Grayson Jones begins to speak from the front of the room. He's the spitting image of Santa Claus, the early years. Joy practically spills out of his ears, and what he lacks in head hair he makes up for with his reddish-brown beard. His smile is infectious and full.

I have a hard time reconciling his joy with the tragedy he reveals in his own life—the loss of his two children to the same boating accident that crippled his wife. How could this man be so full of life?

He has to be a man of prayer.

"Someone once said that we can't be angry with God, because God is never wrong." Grayson paces along the front of the stage, then stops to take a deep breath. "Well, it's true that God is never wrong. And yet we can still get offended and hurt when we don't understand His ways."

I sneak a look at Katie. She's focused on the preacher. I'm running scared inside and my feet are starting to sweat. This man has only uttered a few sentences and already I feel like I'm being singled out. Craning my neck, I check to see if there's a neon arrow pointing at me from above.

"We can get offended with God, just like David did in 2 Samuel 6. Let's go there."

I'm comforted by the familiar sound of Bible pages rustling as people flip to the passage at hand.

"David is returning the ark of the Lord to Jerusalem," Grayson says. "David has been God's anointed one for a long time. He knows God's ways. He's familiar with them. And yet David fails to bring back the ark in the proper way, the way outlined in the book of Deuteronomy. There, God decreed that the ark should be carried by four priests, bearing it on two rods. Instead, David puts the ark on a cart and has thirty thousand worshippers sing high praises to God. He came to fetch it with pomp and ceremony. Imagine the music, the voices, the instruments playing in harmony. Verse five says that they were playing on instruments made out of wood, harps, stringed instruments, tambourines, and cymbals—it was a full blown orchestra. Imagine the sound of unity and rejoicing as the Lord's presence was returned to the people. David spared no expense. Suddenly, the oxen stumble and the ark almost slips off. Uzzah tries to steady it and instead is struck dead for what seems like a thoughtful gesture." Grayson raises his eyebrows. "Why?"

Everyone waits for him to continue, even the girl in front of me.

Grayson brings his hands together in a prayer-like gesture and rests the tips of his fingers against his lips. "Here is the truth: no amount of praise and worship and good intentions can cover up disobedience. It didn't work for David, and it won't work for you."

The room is still. The sound of a baby starting to cry comes from behind me.

My heart beats fast. All of this is hitting too close to home. I want to run, but I'm trapped in my seat. Tears burn my eyes. So much for my dream of wearing mascara in public.

"So, David has a drama queen moment. He starts to pout in verse nine, asking, 'How can the ark of the Lord come to me?' That doesn't sound like any of us, right? We are never heard to be asking, 'How are things ever supposed to change? How can things ever be salvaged?'"

I join in the hesitant, self-conscious laughter.

"Instead of repenting and saying he's sorry for wanting to do it his way, David has a hissy fit. He sends the ark to Gath, a Philistine city, a city David hates. I think David secretly hoped that the people of Gath would get killed from disease and plague like the other Philistine cities. Then it would at least be useful in some sense to him. But instead of revenge on Gath, God blesses the house of Obed-Edom. God pours blessing out on this place, evoking jealousy in David, a jealousy to return to the presence of the Lord. When David hears of the blessing happening at Gath, he changes his heart. He returns the ark the proper way prescribed in Deuteronomy. And he does it rejoicing."

I squirm in my seat and stare at my shoes.

"David thought he could get away with disobedience because he had good intentions. When things didn't happen the way he planned, instead of looking at himself and his sin, he got angry with God. He got so offended that he sent the presence of God away from himself and returned to Jerusalem empty-handed. But God, in His goodness, in His kindness, poured out blessings in Gath and drew David back to Himself.

"God loves you. He loves you and He won't let you get away with disobedience. He'll let you fight and struggle against Him until you finally say, 'I'm tired. I give up. I'll do it Your way.' We can get bitter and whine and complain all we want, but God won't change. God wants us to repent for being angry with Him and for misunderstanding His ways. We've been so angry with God that we haven't wanted His presence. Like David, we've pushed it away. We've been hurt. We need to forgive. He wants us to forgive ourselves, and those who have wounded us, hurt us, and used us.

"Our bitterness and unforgiveness will not get us to a place of peace. If you're more committed to your problems than to God's grace, you'll stay where you are. You need to forgive, otherwise you'll become hard inside, convinced things will never change."

Grayson walks up the aisle and for a brief moment looks right at me. The next words sound in my head like an alarm clock: "You are not stuck."

The air leaves my lungs and I feel punched in the gut.

"You have become angry with God and refused to forgive the things God has asked you to forgive." He takes a deep breath. "You are not stuck. *You are unwilling.*"

Aunt Thuy and Katie both bow their heads. It seems as though, collectively, the whole church has their head bowed. I am overwhelmed. Bowing my head right now feels too much like hanging my head in shame.

I stare up at the ceiling and the black speakers suspended from the rafters. I try to imagine that I'm face to face with my nail-scarred King, but I can't focus. I need to fall and grab Jesus' robe like the woman with the issue of blood. I slip to the ground.

My knees hit the floor first. I press my forehead into the carpet. It smells like fibre and dirt. I cry out to the Lord using all the tears available to me.

"I am sorry, Lord. I thought I was stuck. All this time, I've been believing a lie. I haven't wanted to face the truth. I've been unwilling. I've been blaming You and withholding forgiveness from myself, Ben, and so many others. I'm sorry for not building You an altar of thanksgiving. I'm sorry for refusing to bless Your Name. Forgive me for my good intentions, for believing that eventually I would come around but being unwilling to make You the priority of my heart. Forgive me, Lord. I choose to thank You right now. I choose to thank You for who You are. You are my God and I love You."

I look up, wiping my nose on my shirt. Salty tears slip into my mouth. The feet of the mother and daughter sitting in front of me are mere inches from my face. The girl's backpack rests against her legs.

I freeze.

At this close proximity, I see the tell-tale slash marks of razor cuts.

Chapter Fifteen

My hands feel clammy. Grossest feeling ever. It doesn't matter how many times I wipe my hands on my pants, they continue to sweat. Clenching my fists doesn't help, either. Taking a deep breath, I mutter a prayer and take a step. What am I doing?

The girl from church is by the playground. She makes a move to settle into the swing, but then keeps walking.

"Hey! You there."

You there? What am I, some old lady calling for help to cross the street? What's next? I'll refer to her as "dear."

God, You should have found someone else to do this.

The girl turns. "Yeah?"

"Hey," I try to smile brightly. "I saw you inside the chapel. You were sitting in front of me with your mom."

She stares at me, waiting for me to get to the point.

"I'm Emma. I was wondering if I could talk to you for a minute."

Her posture says, "Duh! What do you think we are doing?" but her eyes search mine for a deeper reason.

I point towards the bench and ask if she wants to sit down.

"I'm not supposed to talk to strangers." Her voice drips with attitude and I suddenly miss Andrea.

I take a chance and walk over to the bench. "I don't bite."

The crunch of gravel behind me tells me she's following. She stands a few feet away as I sit.

She grabs the straps of her backpack. I wonder if she's thinking about the blades I know she keeps inside there. Somehow I know she's the type of girl who needs her supplies by her side at all times. Some cutters only cut in the safety of their bedrooms or bathroom. Others take their blades everywhere. You never know when anxiety could reach an all-time high and you need instant relief.

"How old are you?"

"I'm fifteen. But I'm not Taylor Swift's type of fifteen. I'm just fifteen."

"Country music proves itself useful once again," I say with a lilt. The girl is oblivious to my comment, possibly engaged in concocting a fake excuse about having to meet her mother. "I want to tell you about my life when I was fifteen."

"Go ahead. It's a free country."

"I used to cut myself," I blurt out.

Great job, Emma. Way to ease into things.

Her hazel eyes stare at me hard. There are a few intense seconds of silence before she says, "So?"

I study my hands for a minute. Have I misjudged the situation? I feel a tug inside me and know God is nudging me to say more. "I don't tell my story to just anyone. I need to have a willing audience. Are you willing?"

"Maybe."

The mountains surrounding us invite me to head for the hills and forget this divine appointment. Instead, I open up.

"My mom left us when I was thirteen. It was a few days after school started. I remember that I was really excited because the girls at school had invited me to a sleepover. I raced off the bus and up our sidewalk."

I close my eyes. This story never gets easier. With each telling, the colours seem more vivid. I can feel the wind against my face and my curls caressing my cheeks as I run to the front door.

"The door was open and I could hear my mom laughing."

I stop talking, remembering. Her laugh is like chimes moved by a sudden wind.

"What happened?" the girls asks.

"She didn't see me, but I heard her. I wanted to surprise her and jump out of the closet and scare her. I liked to play tricks on her." I twist my necklace between my fingers, suddenly missing my mom and her laughter. "She had taken a job as a flight attendant a few years before. Travelling made her happy. We saw less of her, though, which made us angry and stressful. We missed her, but our attempts at telling her ended with us fighting or ignoring each other. It just seemed like I was always ticking her off. She started taking extra layover days and visiting all sorts of cool places.

"Anyway, there I was, crouched in the closet, smelling my daddy's leather jacket when I heard her on the telephone. 'No, you heard me, Cindy. I'm not coming back this time. They won't miss me. They don't even love me. They only need me. All the time, they need something from me. And it isn't enough what I give to them. This is a chance of a lifetime and I'm not throwing it away. It's a chance to be happy for once.'"

The girl's eyes are large. "She left you? Did she ever come back?"

This part of the story pierces me as sharply as the girl's question. It doesn't matter how often I tell it.

"No. She never came back."

A robin in the nearby trees starts singing a song. The chirping would be sweet and melodic if it didn't seem so out of place.

"Is that why you cut?"

"It was the starting point. Anxiety was my companion while I hid in the closet. Fear took root inside me. It started as a seed and grew for two years, when a few more messy things happened with her and my dad. It became unbearable. I had an overwhelming need to get the pain out. I was too numb to feel emotion, but the pain in my heart was real. Tears wouldn't come, and neither would words. The bite of the blade seemed to speak for me. My blood poured out like the tears that had been locked away. A sense of power and control came over me. Finally, I could decide when my heart would get hurt. It would be on my terms and no one else's."

Time gives way and the past becomes tangible. I can hear, see, smell the inside of that closet. I feel like I'm still huddled there, watching my mother pick up her suitcase and head for the door while humming the *Love Boat* theme song. That's when rejection set in.

"How did you know I cut?"

The girl's voice startles me out of a private moment. I study her face, incredibly young and beautiful. She has no idea how beautiful she is, though. How could such a young girl carve herself up?

"What's your name?" I ask.

"Vicki."

"That's a great name." I flip my hair behind my shoulder. "I saw some scars and fresh cuts on your ankles when I was in the sanctuary."

Vicki eyes her sneaker-clad feet. "Impossible."

"Possible." I explain how I had ended up facedown in worship, only to find the shock of my life.

Vicki crosses her arms and sits back. "I don't believe you."

"You don't have to believe me. I'm just telling you what happened." We grow silent. I let a few minutes pass. "Tell me about your blade."

She uncrosses her arms. Leaning forward, she grips the edge of the bench. Stealing a look at me, I know she's assessing how much she can risk. "My blade's name is Ben."

I wasn't expecting that cold bucket of water. I regain my breath and manage to squeak out, "Ben?"

"Yeah. I named my blade. We moved this year. All my old friends have boyfriends and I figured, why not me? I don't have any new friends, so whenever one of my old friends asks where I am, I can say I'm with Ben."

I don't know what to say to that.

"Ben makes me feel better. Ben understands what it's like to have everyone in your life be too busy for you."

Vicki grows quiet. Her shoulders slump.

"Thanks for letting me in, Vicki."

"Are you going to tell my mom?"

Vicki's eyes are hard to read. I'm not sure if it's hope or fear in her eyes.

"She needs to know, Vicki. You need help. Ben can't be part of your life forever." If I was an authority on any subject, it was this one. "It's your choice, though. You can tell her or I can."

"What if I'm not ready for her to know?" Vicki started to chew on the side of her thumb.

"Your mom already knows."

She looks up at me sharply. "No, she doesn't."

"That's not what I mean. I mean, your mom already knows something is going on with you. She may not know that you cut, but she knows something's off."

"She doesn't even care about me."

I shook my head. "Believe me, Vicki, I know what it's like to have a mother who doesn't give a rip about you. Your mom cares. You might not know how to communicate with each other, but everything about her says she cares."

"She's just going to try and fix me. She'll make it all about herself and how she has failed as a mother. But it has nothing to do with her, you know?"

"I know. You can't control how she responds. You have to own up to your actions, though."

Vicki groans. "This totally sucks."

"It does. But it gets easier." I reach over, but Vicki takes a step back. Sighing, I put my hands in my lap. "Vicki, have you considered how much God loves you?"

"Not another Sunday school lesson."

"I wasn't supposed to be here today. I'm only here because my friend needed a ride to her aunt's house. That aunt brought me to a chapel service I didn't really want to go to. That chapel service spoke truth that convicted my heart so much that bowing my head in prayer wasn't enough. I had to bow low to the ground. And when I did, I saw you and your scars. God could have picked anyone to talk to you about quitting the blade, but He chose me—a girl who used to cut, a girl whose heart has been recently broken by a guy named Ben." Tears spring to my eyes as I consider the goodness of God. "Trust me when I tell you that Ben can't heal the hurt you have."

I can't believe those words just came out of my mouth.

Vicki's blue eyes stare at me, her face a mixture of emotion. She tugs on the straps of her backpack and I'm certain she's about to leave.

"God knows you, Vicki. He knows every detail about you, even the name of your blade. And He brought me here for this exact moment. God wants you to trust Him. He wants You to trust Him to heal your heart."

A lot of personal revelation is raging inside me, but I'll have to think about it later. I pray fervently, hoping that what I'm saying is the right thing.

Vicki stares at the bench. "I don't know what to do."

I know the next step is to tell her mother. Vicki knows it, too, but I wait. This needs to be her own idea.

"Will you come with me?" she says quietly.

"Yes."

"What if they take Ben away? I can't give him up, Emma. What if…"

"God will give you the strength to survive. It won't be easy. It's a day-by-day journey. You'll start here." I point to the bench. "But each day and each step will take you farther. Until you're there." I point to the highest mountain. "And when you're at the top, you'll look back and see all that you've conquered with Christ. From that perspective, it will make sense."

I should be writing this stuff down!

Vicki laughs shakily. "I don't want to do this, but I don't want you to do this for me, either. What will I say?"

"The truth. However messy and sloppy it comes out, just tell your mom the truth."

We stare at each other. She's scared.

"Do you want to pray?" I ask.

"No, but you can."

I bow my head and thank God for all He has been up to. "For the next steps we take, Lord, we trust You."

Chapter Sixteen

After church, I turn down the chance to stare at a metaphor. Aunt Thuy and Katie want to tour the Hungry Horse dam. Staring at manmade concrete walls holding back the natural flow of water hits a little too close to home for me. Instead I opt for a nap, to recover from church.

The bedroom's wallpaper features a delicate rose pattern, with intricate vines twisting alongside broad leaves and full blooms. It's beautiful, but my thoughts refuse to settle on it. I can't let go of the look on Vicki's face while we spoke with her mother.

My mind starts to mix up scenarios. Instead of picturing Vicki's mother, I see my dad's face and the deep sadness that filled his eyes when he confronted me about cutting. Some memories carry so much emotion that they have the power to crush me.

My eyes grow hot with tears as I think about what's ahead for Vicki. Will her journey be anything like mine? Will her parents get her counselling at church only to find her growing more risky and dark with her self-mutilation over time? Will Vicki alienate her family to the point where her dad has to take six weeks off work? Will she make her grandmother cry? Will her family come to the point where they have to drop her off at a Christian Girls Home to receive around-the-clock care and counselling for fifteen months?

I pray. I pray that Vicki's story will be filled with freedom and truth. I pray that God will show her parents how to handle the situation, that they'll find the best help the first time around. I pray Vicki will give up the blade for good—

—just like I have to give up on my idea of Ben. How long have I used his love to medicate my own soul? When did my dependence shift away from God? Now that Ben is gone, I'm bloody and exposed. Raw.

Let go.

Pretending I'm deaf won't work with God. His whisper is already making its way through my heart. I have a feeling this is one of those moments where I need to do something whether I feel like it or not— like driving the speed limit.

"God…" My voice is shaky. "I'm sorry for making Ben an idol in my heart. I let his love meet my needs in unhealthy ways. Please forgive me, Lord."

With that confession out of the way, the next part comes a bit easier.

"Jesus, I choose to let Ben go." My throat burns with each word. "I release Ben into Your hands and ask that You would heal my heart."

Forgive.

That request sounds a little bit like cleaning up the bathroom after the sewer backs up.

A guttural sob leaves my mouth as the truth rushes in. I don't want to forgive Ben for leaving me. My tragedy defines me right now. It's my identity. I am broken-hearted. As soon as I forgive him, that identity will have to change.

The crying hurts my body. It's full and ripe. I didn't know I was capable of so many tears. This is turning into a Hallmark movie. I need to stop.

"Lord, make me willing. Show me who I am if I let go of this."

The sound is as soft as a blanket covering me: *My daughter.*

"Lord, let me be satisfied in knowing that I'm Your daughter, and that You love me. I choose to forgive Ben." The tears begin anew. "I forgive him for leaving me, for rejecting me. I forgive him for shutting me out of his life, for not giving me any reason for leaving."

The pillow on this bed will need to be wrung out like a mop when I'm done here.

"I forgive him, Lord. I forgive him for hurting my heart, for breaking my trust, for leaving me with a bunch of bills to pay for a wedding that never happened. I was left alone to face all these questions. No one came to my rescue." My breath is ragged, but I'm starting to calm down. "What he did mattered, God. What he didn't do mattered, too. I choose to forgive him. I forgive him for rejecting me, and in its place I receive the gift of being Your daughter. Show me what that means. Help me to be willing. For all the places where I'm stuck, help me be willing to let go and know what it means to be Your daughter."

———————

I'm flipping through my Bible when Katie's text appears two hours later: *We're picking up dinner. Pizza or chicken wings?*

Both, I type back. I have room for a lot of food now that I've emptied out my heart and head.

Clutched in my hand is a rock I picked up when I was with Vicki. I don't know why I reached for it. It seemed like a natural thing to do.

But the more I consider it, the more I understand. I started with a single rock—the one Papa gave me—and now I have a second. Maybe I can build an altar.

The rock is grey and round. It's bigger than a pebble but smaller than a stone. I decide to write a scripture on the rock, the way Papa marked the one he gave me.

I grab a permanent marker from Aunt Thuy's drawer. On one side of the rock, I write out a reminder of this afternoon's message: 2 Samuel 6:10. I like that scripture. It's David being stubborn, and I can relate to that.

He was not willing to take the ark of the Lord to be with him in the City of David. Instead, he took it to the house of Obed-Edom the Gittite.

Turning the rock over, I write Psalm 51:12 in bold print. I'm going to memorize this scripture. I turn the words over in my mouth and let their sound fill my ears:

Restore to me the joy of your salvation and grant me a willing spirit, to sustain me.

I'm in definite need of some sustaining. Not to mention sustenance. Where are the chicken wings and pizza?

I text Katie and she answers that they should be back in ten minutes. That's enough time for me to decorate the table lavishly. As odd as it sounds, I feel like celebrating.

Chapter Seventeen

Layers of mist dress the mountains in lacy white. A cup of tea keeps me company as I contemplate their magnitude. Snuggling into the corner of the porch swing, I draw warmth from the cup in my hands and drink in the fresh morning air. It's the type of morning Ben would love. If this had been our home, I would be sitting here, waiting for him to return from a morning run.

But it isn't my home, and Ben isn't coming.

During a walk after dinner last night, I thought I saw Ben on the street. It turned out instead to be a man named Jordan who sold mounted deer heads and bait tackle. I lost a vanilla ice cream cone over the shock.

I'd hoped that all my feelings for Ben would magically disappear after the previous day's prayer, like morning mist under a hot sun. No such luck. Ben is still gone and it hurts like hell.

The screen door creaks open and Aunt Thuy, wrapped in a purple housecoat that boasts "I'm the Queen of this Castle." Her ample behind drops into the swing and sets it in motion. Her eyes are closed, relaxed.

A question that has been idling at the back of my mind presses forward. Asking it will make me feel foolish, and yet the answer will be crucial.

"Aunt Thuy…" I angle myself towards her. She opens her dark eyes and looks straight at me—through me. "I'd like to ask you something."

"No, I won't give you the recipe for the meal I made yesterday."

I blink twice. "Uh, no. That's not what I'm after."

Aunt Thuy considers this for a moment. Have I insulted her by not asking for it? Taking a sip of tea, I wonder how to be tactful. Maybe it's best to approach this the Vietnamese way-—direct and to the point.

"Are you happy? Are you happy being single, having been single for most of your life?"

Aunt Thuy eyes me shrewdly, having discerned my real intent. I'm really asking if I'll be happy if I never get married, if I end up single and the only children in my life are my niece and nephew.

"No."

The teacup in my hand trembles.

"And yes." Aunt Thuy gives the swing a gentle push. "Marriage is hard work, or so I've observed. But being single is hard work, too, sometimes."

"What do you mean?"

"There are days when you're alone and it snows and no one will go outside to warm up the car for you. There are times when you want to show little hands how to wrap a spring roll, but there's no one. There are days when it's dark and lonely."

I stare at the potted zinnias and wish I had never asked my question.

"But there are also days when you realize you can offer your home to travellers like yourself and feed them good food. On these days, your house will be filled with chatter and you will be full. When everyone leaves, you'll sit in your quiet house and say, 'Yes. I like this best. This quiet.' After all, sometimes lonely is just quiet in disguise."

I ponder this for a moment. "Isn't it hard, though? To surrender your dream of being loved? Of being held in a man's arms and hearing his voice soothe you?"

I've crossed from Aunt Thuy's reality to the present fear of mine. What if Ben was my only chance at love? What if I only got to taste love without being able to eat the whole pie?

Aunt Thuy gives me a pointed look. "God's grace is enough."

I hate her answer. I didn't ask her these questions to be placated. I want the nitty-gritty details of being single. How does she handle everyone's nosy questions? Does she cry herself to sleep at night? Is chocolate a true substitute for the love of a good man?

"Emma, now it's my turn to ask the questions. What is it you're after?"

I study the rose on my teacup. Words swim around my head and try to line up in order. I'm not sure where to start.

"I just want..." I hesitate. It sounds silly in my head. "I just want the pain to stop."

"Is that all you want?"

I narrow my eyes. Is she making fun of me? "What do you mean? Should there be more?"

"Well, let's say you get this wish of yours—all the pain is gone. What will you have learned about God?"

I tuck a loose strand of hair behind my ear. "I guess I would learn that He's my deliverer. That He's able to rescue me."

"Is that all?"

I tilt my head to the side, curious to know where this conversation is heading. "I guess so."

"What if there's more, Emma? What if God wants you to know Him as more than the Prince Charming who rides in and saves the day? What if He wants you to know Him as a Healer and Restorer, as the Good Shepherd who guides you through dark valleys? The real question is this: do you want to know God for who He really is?"

The neighbour's car starts. Two joggers pass, disappearing down the street.

"Yes." My voice is quiet and doesn't sound like my own. "Yes, I do."

"Then I would encourage you to give up this ridiculous genie-in-a-bottle type of prayer. Stop asking for deliverance and start asking for guidance. Knowing God and His character means having to pass through the valley. There will be no helicopter evacuation. You're going to have to go through this one step at a time."

"I don't like the sound of that."

Aunt Thuy's dark eyes find mine. "You silly girl. You're only thinking of the pain you might encounter. You're supposed to look up and gaze upon Him. The beauty of Jesus eclipses pain so you can walk towards the joy set before you." She looks me over, then declares, "There will be days when it hurts, but then you'll encounter His healing and peace. And when you encounter it often enough, your heart will be settled and whole again."

The sun's brilliance lights up the yard. The blooming hydrangea bushes dance beneath the bold touch of sunshine. The soft morning hush grants Aunt Thuy's comments special reverence.

"His grace is sufficient?" I ask.

She sets her feet on the porch, stopping the swing. "His grace is sufficient."

———

When Katie first became a meaningful part of my life, I hated her. I filled pages in my journal with angry rants about her, declarations of revenge and dreams of her public humiliation, including one particularly funny one involving a weasel, maple syrup, and hair dye.

Katie is actually the person who ratted me out and exposed the truth about my cutting habit in high school. We didn't know each other very well, but she knew the signs of a cutter. Her older sister had been one and their family had gone through its own personal hell. When Katie found me cleaning a wound in the bathroom at school, she didn't buy my story that I'd cut myself at home and was just re-bandaging it.

Her eyes were on me for the next few days. Somehow I knew she was in on my secret. I also knew she would tell.

And she did.

I hated her for it. I despised her and wrote poems about how I was going to glue her fingers to her forehead. I even refused to see her the first time she tried to visit me at the Girls Home. It took an hour to drive there and I wanted her to be disappointed that her little charity visit hadn't turned out the way she planned. I watched out the window as she retreated to her car, her black hair falling over bowed head. I gave her the finger, though I doubt she saw it.

My anger came in many forms.

A month later, she returned. I had softened a bit and was desperate to see a new face, so this time I let her in. Our conversation was awkward, stilted. At the end of the visit, she gave me a gift: five handmade cue cards with scriptures on them. Each card had a scripture about hope.

She literally brought me hope that day.

Today, she's going to get in a car with Aunt Thuy and drive away to her future. I'm not sure I'm ready to let go. Letting go isn't my strong suit.

"Emma?"

Katie's voice brings me back to the moment. I'm in the bathroom, staring into the mirror over the vanity. "Yeah?"

"Are you crying?"

"No," I lie. I check the bathroom door and make sure it's locked.

"So, you'll cry over Ben, but not over me!?"

I snort.

"Anyway, Aunt Thuy says there's time for a quick walk."

I wipe my eyes and unlock the door, only to be greeted by Katie's black hair and a big grin.

We walk down a path in front of Aunt Thuy's place. The trees shroud us and the delphiniums keep us company.

"Are you excited?" I ask.

"Yes. I'm a bit nervous about finding a place, though. I keep kicking myself, thinking I should have moved before the end of the month, but my plans didn't work out that way."

"Plans, plans, plans," I mutter.

Katie laughs. "We're foolish aren't we, Em, to think that our lives will follow our plans?"

"I don't know about foolish. Maybe just hopeful."

She shrugs. "I'm going to miss you, Patch."

I freeze with my mouth open. "You swore you would never bring that up again."

"Maybe I lied."

"You are horrible!"

"I'm not the one who didn't shave her legs properly and then spent a weekend camping with our friends with a patch of leg hair the size of Texas, now did I?"

I stare at her, sputtering, hands on my hips. "Shut it, Peeping Katie!"

Katie shakes her head. "You peep once and no one forgets. I didn't realize it was the men's bathroom."

We burst into fits of laughter recounting how Katie once came out of a bathroom stall only to shock a man in his seventies who had just entered.

"Hey, wait." I reach into the back pocket of my jeans. "Here's a gift for you."

Katie's almond eyes open wide. "Emma, you've already given me tons of stuff. And you drove me here. Do you know how invaluable that is?"

"Whenever you need me, I'll be there." I extend my gift towards her.

She reaches for the stack of cards in my open hand. I wait for the recognition on her face.

Her breath catches. "You still have these after all these years?"

"I've always had them. I thought you could use them while you start your new life. You know, to help you choose to be hopeful instead of feeling foolish."

Katie stares at me, then looks down at the three-by-five cue cards covered with promises of hope.

For You have been my hope, O Sovereign Lord, my confidence since my youth. (Psalm 71:5)

Katie smiles at me. "It's true, Emma. He's our hope, isn't He?"

"He's the One we can trust."

She stands back. "You are different. Something has happened to you this weekend."

I relate the abridged version of the church service, my encounter with Vicki, the afternoon spent in prayer, and my conversation with Aunt Thuy. The retelling brings us back to the front porch.

"Emma Carmichael, you're going to be just fine without me."

"It won't be as much fun, though."

"True. What will you do?" We laugh and embrace. "I'm going to miss you."

"Me too, Katie."

Just then, Aunt Thuy hustles out the door and down the steps, carrying a brown bag. "Here, Emma."

"An autographed picture of Reba McIntyre? I can't believe you're giving this to me."

Aunt Thuy looks around. "Well, Mel hasn't missed it the way I thought he would. If he hasn't come for it by now, he's never going to."

I throw my arms around her. "Thank you," I whisper. "And thank you for talking with me this morning."

Aunt Thuy steps back. "Keep in touch."

"I will."

Katie and Aunt Thuy climb into the Honda Civic. Aunt Thuy puts the car in reverse and starts down the driveway. I wave like a five-year-old until the red taillights disappear and Katie is gone from sight.

Rooted to the spot, I take a deep breath. Then I move. I will *not* stand still. I have hope for the future. A new start.

I bend down and pick up a rock.

Chapter Eighteen

I'm currently engaged in my favourite form of entertainment. Where is a bowl of popcorn when you need one? A girl goes away for a few days and the phone lines go crazy!

"Emma."

I cringe at the sound of that voice.

"Mr. MacDonald needs to go for a walk. Also, there's ten dollars here with your name on it if you want to mow my lawn this afternoon. And my garden is in need of watering, maybe you can help me out with that, too."

I don't hear the rest of her message. I'm too busy putting my toothbrush back into the bathroom. For all I know, she's requesting that I caulk her windows and clean out the gutters. Or worse, go inside her house.

Beep.

I open my backpack to sort the laundry.

"Emma," Andrea says. "I need a ride, desperately. Please, please, please, pleaaaaase! And what's with you not answering your cell phone? Call me back. Please."

Wonder of wonders. I go away for a few days and Andrea learns her manners.

Beep.

"Emma, Mrs. MacDonald here again. I have a friend who needs her dog walked, too. Since you're already walking Mr. MacDonald, I figured you could walk the two dogs at the same time. My friend has just had a hip replacement. It would make a huge difference in her life if she knew Champ was keeping *his* hips in better condition. Call me when you get this."

Double cringe.

Beep.

"Hi Emma, Tammy here. Call me. I miss your smiling face. I'd like you to visit me at the Girls Home when you have a chance."

Beep.

"Emma, it's Natalie."

I stop unpacking my bag and walk over to the machine. Was she calling to apologize? Does she miss me?

"Something has happened. Please call me."

My blood goes cold. Is everything okay? My dad... oh no, something has happened to him.

Please, God! Please let Dad be okay. Please. Please. Please.

Now I'm starting to sound like Andrea!

I pick up the phone and dial Natalie's number. Why didn't I text her during the trip? Why did I turn my cell off? A few moments later, I wonder why she isn't picking up.

What has happened?

———

"So you had a fight with Mark?" I say, repeating Natalie's big announcement.

Natalie looks into her tea, her eyes downcast. "Yeah."

"And that was the big 'something's happened' that you left on my machine?" Well, I decide to add a little drama of my own. "Natalie! Do you have any idea how worried I was? I nearly ran over Mr. MacDonald on my way over!"

"Are you sure you weren't aiming for him?"

I throw my head back in exasperation. "Maybe. But that's not the point. I thought something serious happened to Dad or Gigi or Papa or Jack or..."

"Oh, Emma! You've always been such a worry wart. It wasn't *that* serious."

I want to walk out. *This* is my problem with Natalie. She doesn't understand me, and when I try to explain things, she brushes it off. It's so tiring. When she isn't trying to fix me, she acts as if nothing I say has merit.

"Mark and I had a fight," she confirms for the third time, baiting the hook. I know she wants me to ask if everything is okay between them, but I don't bite. I'm not interested in hearing about her petty arguments. "We had a fight about my blog, actually."

Now *that* gets my interest. "Oh?"

"Apparently, Mark and you see things the same way."

"Which way is that?"

Natalie nails me with a look. I sip my tea to hide a growing grin.

"Mark feels that I reveal too much of our personal lives."

"And do you?"

Natalie gulps. "Yeah. I do."

I sit quietly, waiting for the rest of the story to spill out.

"I didn't tell Mark that you and I fought at the library. I was afraid he would agree with you. Then you cancelled babysitting and he asked why he hadn't seen you around lately." She sipped her tea and settled the mug between her hands. "I told him what you said about my blog. He decided to read the entries I wrote. Then he read other entries I'd written about our marriage and family life."

Poor Mark. He's such a private person.

"We got into a big fight over it," Natalie continues. "He was angry with me for exposing our inner lives to strangers. At first, I couldn't understand why he was making such a big deal out of it."

"What changed your mind?"

"He asked me if I was writing all these entries just to get people to comment and say that I was a great person or that I had a great life."

"Were you?"

Natalie rises and walks over to the tea kettle. Her cup doesn't need refilling, but I can sense she needs to feel safe. Standing behind the island counter seems to provide that.

"I denied it at first, storming off in good ol' Natalie fashion. But his criticism made me ask myself some hard questions. Emma, receiving witty comments from strangers is extremely validating! My readers think I'm smart and talented. Someone even suggested that I look like Angelina Jolie in a few of my pictures." Natalie splays her fingers against the counter. "I've been telling myself that this is just a record of my life, but if that were true I would have just journalled instead of posting everything online. In public."

My sister looks fragile and humble. Lonely almost, as though she's truly considering her actions and how they impact others.

"My life doesn't seem so redundant and unfulfilling when I write about it. Somehow I'm able to transform it into this coveted experience. And the comments affirm me and tell me that I'm so blessed to have the life I do."

"Nat, why don't you think your life is great?"

Her lips tremble and she gives me a delicate smile.

"You have a family," I say. My sister's insecurity is news to me. "You're married to the man of your dreams, and he's a good man. You have two adorable kids you get to stay home with and raise. You're a committed and caring mother—a miracle in itself considering what we grew up with. And you're a great sister and friend. You're living the life God has called you to live. Not to mention, you live in Canada, one of the most privileged nations in the world!"

I stop before pointing out the first-world conveniences of running water, electricity, and sanitation. That would be a bit over the top.

"Emma, I know this will sound crazy, but sometimes I just want to get in a car and drive away from it all—just go somewhere new and be like one of those people who starts over in a small town and discovers who they really are."

I am silent. Could my sister be deceived by such a lie? The old notion that life is greener on the other side of the fence?

I shrug. "You aren't our mother, Natalie. You aren't like Nina."

She starts to cry. "What if I am? Emma, I think I understand her. I think I understand why she left us. She was bored and felt like she was missing out on an exciting life. She wanted to do something special, leave her mark on the world."

I stand up and move over to the island. "The only marks she left, Nat, are scars on the hearts of those who loved her. She's selfish. Nothing makes her content, not even the different lives she's tried on since she left. You have to know that."

"My head knows that, but there are days when everything in life drives me up the wall. I love my husband, but he annoys me to no end with his weird habits. I love my kids, but they demand my attention all the time. I love my friends, but I feel like no one ever truly gets me. Some days, the toll of doing the same thing over and over drives me round the bend."

How long has Natalie been feeling this way? Where was I that I couldn't see she needed encouragement? I've been so proud, wanting to be right rather than show love.

I move around the counter and wrap my arms around her. She falls against me and sobs. I've never encountered Natalie in such a vulnerable state. My older sister is strong—a force of nature.

"Everything is going to be okay," I whisper.

"Mom, can I have some crackers?" Jack asks, interrupting our sob fest with his pleading voice.

Natalie lifts her head and wipes her tears.

"I'll take care of it," I offer.

Jack and I locate the box of animal crackers and pour some into a bowl. I head towards the living room with the snack.

"I'm not allowed to eat in the living room," Jack informs me. "It makes a mess."

"This is an Auntie Emma treat," I tell him. "And any mess that is made, Auntie Emma will clean up."

Jack looks at his mom for permission. Natalie nods and says, "Go on."

"Hooray!" Jack shouts, then whispers so as not to wake his sleeping sister. "Was mommy crying?"

"A little," I say as Jack leads me into the living room. "Sometimes it's good to cry."

"And sometimes you cry when you skin your knee on the cement."

"That too." I set the bowl down in front of Jack and turn on the

TV. I know Natalie and I need a few more minutes. I pray silently that another half-hour of TV won't turn his brains to mush.

I return to the kitchen, where Natalie is busy wiping down the counters.

"Come sit," I say.

She sinks into a wooden chair. We let the room fill with silence. I'm in no hurry to rush our conversation.

"God is working in my heart, Emma," she says. "I think God is trying to work on areas I've let grow hard."

Natalie never talks about God like this. In fact, I'm not sure we ever truly talk about how God works in our lives. I usually save those conversations for Katie. I like this, though. I could get used to it.

"One area is my anger towards Nina for leaving us. My animosity has never been loud or demonstrative, not like yours. I used to envy you for cutting yourself."

I shake my head in disbelief. "What?"

"That came out wrong. What I mean is that I used to envy the fact that you were angry enough to let it all out."

"You have it wrong, sis. There was no release for my anger, and that's why I cut. I believed that I had no choice. There was nothing good about the cutting. It never helped me deal with my anger."

"I know. I remember." She heaves a sigh. "When Nina first left, I needed to be strong for you and Daddy. Especially after you started cutting. Then I got caught up in university and my life with Mark. The first few years of marriage have carried me through, but now…"

Natalie dissolves into tears. Getting up, I grab the Kleenex box. It's wonderful to be the one giving tissue rather than receiving it.

"I have these amazing and beautiful children. They love me, depend on me, and forgive me so easily. I just can't help but feel angry and think, 'What kind of mother walks out on her kids?' Then I get scared and think, 'What if I do that? What if I walk away from them? What if I'm just like her?'"

I reach over and once again pull her into a hug. She isn't being dramatic. What she said on the answering machine is true. Something *did* happen. God is softening her heart.

I pray quietly and wonder what to say next. Nothing inspiring comes to mind, so I just let my sister cry.

Natalie blows her nose. "I was just supposed to apologize to you for blabbing about your life on my blog. I didn't expect this."

I look into her soft blue eyes. "I'm glad you told me, Nat. Thank you. And I forgive you for all the blog stuff."

"Yeah, well... I'm a big mess."

"If it's any consolation, you only look like a small mess."

Nat swats my arm. "My anger scares me, Emma. There's a lot of it and it's sucking the joy out of my life. I'm scared and angry. It's affecting my marriage and making me parent like a coward."

I tuck her hair behind her ears and play the role of a big sister for once. "You aren't going to stay in that state, Nat. Just as you said, God is doing something in your life. How fast it gets done is completely up to you, though. Just surrender to Him and cooperate, okay?"

Natalie sits back. "Wow. When did you get to be so wise?"

"I'm not wise, Natalie. I'm just as foolish as anyone. But I finally stopped running this weekend and decided to trust God for the future."

"I'm proud of you."

Those words warm me inside. There's something affirming about your sister telling you she thinks you're doing the right thing. I hope it works with her as well.

"I'm proud of you, too."

Natalie's smile is broad and full. "Do you think God is trying to get both of us to forgive Nina so He can work in her life?"

"I don't know. God is always going to work towards having us live in forgiveness. And He's always going to be at work to woo Nina to Himself." I shift in my chair. "Whatever God is up to, I want to cooperate with it."

"Together?"

I thrill at the promise of friendship with my sister. "Yeah. I'd like that."

We're about to have one of those cheesy moments that happen on made-for-TV movies. Instead, my nephew comes in and announces,

"Hey, Auntie Emma, I crumbled up our cookies and made a dirt floor for you!"

I look at Natalie, who bursts out laughing. "You're on your own, sister," she says.

But for the first time in a long time, I know that isn't true.

Chapter Nineteen

"All right, class, today my challenge for you is to find new and unusual methods of creating art using ordinary objects."

Andrea doodles on her page while I hide my cell phone to read a text from Katie: *Check your email.*

It will have to wait until class is over. Monique is holding up a rubber band and challenging us to stretch our minds for how we can use everyday items in art.

Andrea looks at me with a snarly glare. She's still upset about her boyfriend not showing up to take her to the movies last night. Apparently it was the third time he blew her off.

I defended him and tried to help her see reason. After all, he does have a job landscaping and mowing lawns. Those hours can go late. My use of logic made me the enemy, though, and she told me in verbose terms that I needed to shut up and get a life.

"I want you to try using string, yarn, thumbtacks, spools, combs, whatever you have handy or can find in this room. The idea is for you to find something you're used to using in a particular way and then change it. Let's begin."

I move quickly to the front of the room. Sitting still means that Andrea might come over and complain about her life. I should take an interest, but she exhausts me.

A bale of string is shoved into my hands by Clarke, the class clown. "Release yourself, Emma! Unwind the string and all that pent-up energy you have inside." He wiggles his eyebrows up and down.

Ah, there's nothing like a teenage boy. "If only I were eight years younger, Clarke," I say with a smile on my face. I turn my back to him before he announces that he likes older women and wants me to pose for a painting.

Cutting the string so that it's the same length from my elbow to my hand, I tie one end to the tip of a paintbrush. This idea might not go anywhere, but it's worth a try.

The red paint pours onto the tray in a vibrant and raw hue. Balancing the load carefully, I pass Andrea and her plastic wrap sculpture on the way back to my seat.

"Okay, Jesus. Give me some divine inspiration." Slowly, I dip the string into the paint. I look behind me. The coast is clear.

I wind back my arm, tense for a moment, then surge forward. Just like that, the string becomes a whip.

Splat!

A thin red line lands on the page.

I stand back and look at it. Some residue is spread out in tiny dots around the bold mark. I set my arm back and aim for a different spot on the page. The colour blooms like a rose bursting open.

Monique walks by and says, "I'm interested to see where this will lead, Emma."

You and me both.

A response to my weekend in Montana has been stirring inside me. I have thought a lot about what took place there. I should journal what happens to me, but who am I kidding? I don't journal. Maybe today's assignment will help me sort out my thoughts.

I slap the canvas with another whip-like stroke.

After the fifth stroke, I stop. The five red lines remind me of something.

I gulp.

Cut marks. These look just like the cut marks I used to make on my arm. The last one in particular looks like the kind of cut I made most frequently. I used to slide the blade across the palm of my hand. Not too deep. Just deep enough. It brought instant pain. Logically, I thought, it would be easy to explain away if anyone got suspicious. The truth, though, is that a cut across your hand hurts all day, all night, and any time you use your hands. It's also slow to heal, which is exactly why I did it. If the pain was close to me and I could feel the ache, I could concentrate on it and feel okay for a while. Making a fist kept the anxiety at bay.

Eventually it would heal. A day would come when I'd stare at my hand and run my fingertips across the palm, checking to see if it was mended, if my skin had closed up. I'd think maybe I was better. Maybe I had left enough of an opening for all the heartache to make its way out so I wouldn't need to cut again. Maybe I was okay.

And I was... for a week. Sometimes only a day. Then my emotions would start to bubble inside me and beg for release. I would cut a door for them so they could escape. Each time I hoped they would never come back. Have I always been like that? Have I always been slow to mend so I could experience the pain fully?

I slap the string across the page again, this time making horizontal lines instead of vertical ones. Slowly a cross starts to take shape.

This weekend I realized that God is serious about us doing things His way. I rejected His way of doing things so many times—with Ben and with cutting. I wanted comfort more than I wanted to face the truth. Being comforted became an idol and I did everything I could to get it. Idols are hungry beasts, always demanding a sacrifice. This idol literally demanded my blood and took control of my life. Cutting became religion to me. I would cut with ceremony, devoutly cleaning my blades after every cut. I lived by the rules of my blade.

I whip the page again. The image of the scarred, cut, blood-stained cross is emblazoned on the page.

There's only One who can save. There's only One whose blood is the final sacrifice.

He was wounded for our transgressions. Bruised for our iniquities.

My Saviour was scarred for love's sake. He carries scars on His body to remind me that I don't need any scars of my own. He paid the price.

It is finished.

And so is my painting.

My response to this weekend—all that happened in the service, with Vicki and at Aunt Thuy's house—has found its way onto canvas. I have given up all my old ways of comfort.

Once the area is clean, I remove the string from the paintbrush, tossing it into the garbage on my way to the bathroom.

The tap twists easily and I work up a lather to wash away the paint. Red liquid runs down the drain.

I look at my hands.

I am clean.

———

"I want you to drive me home." Andrea's arms are crossed and her black nails tell me I shouldn't argue with her.

I suppress the urge to kick her out of my car. Since when did manners become obsolete? "No can do, amigo. I have a deal with your mom, and the deal is that I return you to the magazine office."

"I don't want to go there."

I shrug and start the engine.

"You aren't seriously taking me there, are you?"

"I am so seriously taking you there." I bob my head, thinking it will make me look cool and funny. I just feel old.

"Whatever. Do what you're told. You always do."

"Are you going to explain that last remark?" I ask.

I sigh, knowing that one of Andrea's hobbies is to push people's buttons. Maybe I'm naive, but every time she tries I take the bait.

Andrea gives me a look of disgust.

"It's called being responsible, Andrea. I do as I'm asked because I'm being responsible."

"You weren't very responsible at my mom's magazine. That's why you were fired, remember?"

Taking a deep breath, I start a mental count. They say that counting to ten can have a calming effect. I'm up to the number thirty-four when Andrea interrupts me.

"I know you don't like me, Emma. You don't have to keep hanging out with me. Or do you just do that because your life is pathetic and you have nothing else to do?"

If there's a degree for making people feel small, Andrea would have a doctorate. I pray, asking God for wisdom, love, and patience. I may have even asked that He bring back the method of old where He opened the ground and swallowed people up.

"If you're mad at me for not catering to your whims, just say it, Andrea. But don't be cruel because you don't have the guts to be honest."

Huh. I didn't know I was capable of tough talk. All this Dr. Martha stuff is paying off.

Andrea pulls out her phone. "Whatever."

Her sudden gasp is more like a shout from a toddler. Her fingers move quickly, texting. I'm tempted to ask if everything is okay, but I know I won't have to wait long. Andrea can't keep news to herself. Everyone has to hear the top stories as they happen.

She tosses the phone into her lap. "Unbelievable!"

"Hmmmm," I say nonchalantly.

Andrea flips open her compact and checks her hair and makeup. "I can't believe it. I texted Rudy to pick me up from my mom's office." Rudy, the boyfriend who has a job and can't spend every waking minute with Princess Andrea. "And he had the nerve to ask for gas money. What am I to him?"

I like Rudy. I've never met him, but anyone who has a backbone with Andrea is a hero in my books. "Andrea, it's a forty-minute drive. Gas isn't cheap."

"He has a juh-ob," Andrea says.

"I thought you said he was saving for college."

"Yeah, but I'm his girlfriend. Hello?"

This, right here, is why sixteen-year-olds shouldn't date—especially prissy, self-centred sixteen-year-olds.

"Andrea, cut him some slack. He has to earn his way to college. He isn't like you. He doesn't have parents who had his tuition paid for by his ninth birthday. You're an only child who gets what you want, when you want it. Stop being so spoiled. Give Rudy some respect."

"Respect? Ugh! He doesn't show me any respect. Respect is earned, Emma. If you knew that, you probably wouldn't have let that Ben guy break your heart. He probably had no respect for you at all. What a jerk. All men are jerks. Rudy is a jerk. Ben is a jerk."

Okay. Here's where I lay down the law. You can talk bad about your life and your guy, but don't you dare comment on my man.

Or ex-man. Semantics.

I park in the lot of the magazine office and lock the doors so Andrea can't escape.

"Andrea, you know nothing. You know nothing of the type of man Ben is and you know nothing about why he broke off our engagement. You have no right to call him names when he has only been a good, loving, kind, and generous man. You are my cousin and family. I love you, but I won't put up with your crap attitude or bad-mouthing good people. You're angry because you aren't getting your way. Don't take it out on me. Toughen up."

My words fall on deaf ears. Andrea tugs at the door handle. "Are you going to let me out?"

I give her a steely look. At least, I think it's steely.

"Whatever," rolls out of her mouth again. "Just let me out, Emma."

"Not until you apologize."

"What?"

"You aren't going anywhere until you apologize to me."

"For what?"

"For being rude. For taking your anger out on me. For using me to take you to art class because you're too lazy to take the bus. I deserve an apology."

Andrea's nostrils flare. "No."

"Okay, then. Buckle up." I put the car in drive and hit the gas pedal.

Andrea screams at me. "What are you doing?"

To be honest, I have no idea. All I know is that I'm tired of being walked on. I will *not* be a doormat.

Andrea dials her cell phone. "Mom, Emma has totally lost it. She won't let me out of the car." The car is momentarily silent as she listens to her mom. "What do you mean what did I do? I did nothing. Emma is a lunatic."

I slam on the brakes at the far end of the parking lot. Andrea grabs the lock and hops out of the car. "You're totally crazy," she says.

"Have fun walking back."

I think she's saying something foul to me, but I can't be sure. I simply crank up my country music and leave her in the dust.

Chapter Twenty

MochaJanova's has a soothing atmosphere. I need something to help me calm down after saying goodbye to Andrea. Something topped with whipped cream usually does the trick.

I'm also eager to check my email and see what Katie sent. I miss having a sane friend.

Already the whipped cream is working its magic. I'm even patient while I wait for my computer to accept my password. Countless spam invitations for shopping, starting a new business, and becoming a travel writer beg for my attention. I delete them and filter out the weekly and monthly updates from my favourite websites. In total I have four actual emails.

The first one is from my dad. There's a photo of him completely covered in mud. According to the email, the kids of Nicaragua coaxed him to join their mud fight. He lost.

The next email is from Katie. Attached are photos of her little apartment and a hilarious story about her neighbour's dog. Apparently, she has a neighbour who's as crazy as mine. Now we can swap crazy neighbour stories.

The third email is a surprise.

Dear Emma,
We cannot thank you enough for helping Vicki this past

weekend in Montana. We were suspicious that something was going on in her life, but we didn't know for sure.

I wanted to email to tell you that Vicki has agreed to go into counselling. This has been a very dark week for our family, but there is hope in God and we are clinging to that.

Please keep in touch with our family. We will forever be grateful for the role God had you play in Vicki's life this past weekend.

Many prayers and blessings, sincerely,

Patricia DeLuca

The words blur in front of me as I wipe tears from my eyes. I'm such a mess today. Pull it together, Carmichael.

This next email better make me laugh, because all the whipped cream is gone from my drink, leaving nothing to refresh me.

Dear Emma,

How are you? I miss you like crazy beans! We have to talk soon—it's been too long! What is your new phone number?

Your bridesmaid dress is all ready and we can do the alterations when you come to the wedding shower. It's a week and a half away, can you believe it? You are still coming, right? Please?

When you come, I'm taking you out for lunch and we're going to have some girl time. We don't have to talk about Ben—unless you want to. I just want to see my Emma-girl. And you are staying at our new place! Greg and I just moved all our belongings (which wasn't much!) into our new apartment. I'm living in it and setting everything up before the wedding. I can't wait to show you.

I've been praying for you. It was great talking with you a few weeks ago. How's the job at your aunt's magazine going? Let me know how life is going in Emma land.

Missing you like crazy,

—the soon-to-be Mrs. Riverton (Mandy!!!!!!)

I used to sign my emails like that, too, only it was "the soon-to-be Mrs. Benjamin Fenton." How did I end up here? How did I end up in an internet cafe with a cold mocha and a computer for company on a Friday afternoon?

My head starts to hurt as I long for home.

I quickly reply to Mandy with my home number rather than my cell. I love Mandy, but I can't risk her giving my cell number to Ben. Not that he would ask for it, if she even knows where he is. Still… if I'm going to have a conversation with him, I don't want it happening by surprise.

As I hit send, I see a P.S. tag at the bottom of Mandy's email that I missed the first time around. I reopen the email and skip to the bottom, past the signoff:

PS. Check out my photos on Facebook—you will not believe it!!!

I check the time on the computer and see that I have four minutes left. I open Facebook and note that I haven't updated my status in over ten weeks. My last status update was: *I'm taking a break from Facebook.*

I check Mandy's page, then scroll down to the date on which she sent the email. There's a picture of the inside of her wrist with a tattoo of white lilies wrapped in blue ribbons.

What in the world? I click on the picture to enlarge it. In scripted letters, it reads: "Something new and blue… for my wedding day. Anyone have something old I can borrow?"

I sit back and laugh. It's classic Mandy.

Scanning Mandy's newsfeed to catch up on what's happening in the lives of our other mutual friends and acquaintances, I search for Ben's name.

Halfway down, I find a fairly new status: *Enjoying the burritos here in Mexico and hoping the vendor washed his hands before making them.*

Huh? I click on Ben's profile and hope it will reveal more. The page comes to life with comments and updates for the past five days.

All we have is a dial-up connection here in Mexico. Just wanted to say we're here and we're alive… Hi Mom! ;)

What? Who is this "we"? I scroll past all the responses, looking for more information. Something dated last week sheds light on the whole issue: *I'm about to get on a plane to Mexico! Three cheers for my cousin's youth group. Tacos... here we come!*

Suddenly, my screen goes blank. An announcement appears stating that my session is over. Instead of moving, my jaw hangs open wide enough for birds to roost in it.

Ben, my Ben, is in Mexico. Mexico!

From the dates on his page, he has been there for a week and a half. He's out of the country and I was clueless about it.

I hate Facebook.

My brain starts to put the pieces together of where and who Ben is with. I know his cousin Randy was going to Mexico on a missions trip. Ben and I had contributed to his fundraising efforts—twenty meagre dollars from our wedding's savings account.

"Excuse me. Are you done with the computer?" A teenage boy with a backwards baseball cap waits anxiously. "I'm next."

"Oh, right. I'm all done here. I just need to collect my things."

"Cool. Thanks."

"Yeah." I say, stunned. "Cool."

———

Later, while filling my car with gas, I have an epiphany. I figure out the *real* reason Ben has gone to Mexico. It's obvious, isn't it? He's moving on with his life. A life that was supposed to include me now includes rice and beans. And that's going up in the world.

I finish pumping the gas, screw the lid back into place, and slam the door shut.

He's probably going to meet some seniorita down there. Someone with a great complexion, an infectious laugh, and dark, luminous eyes. The women there always have luminous eyes. And I bet she'll be really curvy and have black hair. She'll help orphans and feed her ailing grandmother while weaving baskets to make a better life for her siblings.

I can't compete with that. I don't even have an ailing grandmother. He's probably already forgotten me and what he once called "the kindest eyes I've ever seen."

Ugh!

He's moving on. Without me.

I stalk towards the gas station door and yank it open. Now is the time to do something bold. Something rash.

Marching over to the freezer bin, I wrap both hands around a tub of Häagen-Dazs. "I'm buying this, too."

"Okay," the clerk with dreadlocks says slowly. He fails to notice my life-altering purchase and watches me sign the credit card receipt before returning to watch a soap opera on the tiny TV mounted in the corner of the store.

"That kind of stuff will rot your brain out," I warn him. I leave before he can thank me for my sage wisdom.

Chapter Twenty-One

I just ate an entire carton of ice cream. In my defence, it was mint chocolate chip again. It's a known fact that peppermint has been used for centuries to restore the soul. It just so happens that it goes down a whole lot smoother with chocolate.

The phone rings and I ignore it. My answering machine whirrs to life.

"Emma, this is Mrs. MacDonald." I pull a blanket over me, deciding that I need sleep. "Emma dear, I know you're screening this call. Your car is in the driveway and you came into the house with a pint of ice cream earlier. I may be old, but I'm not stupid."

Or blind, apparently.

"You're wallowing, aren't you? Well, I don't have time for that. I need you to take Mr. MacDonald out for his walk right now. I'm needed elsewhere. I will see you here in five minutes. Toodles!"

I roll over in bed and punch my pillow.

Well, I need to do something to get in shape. If I'm ever going to see Ben again, it's not going to be with a whole dairy cow living in the pasture of my behind.

———

Mr. MacDonald put me through my paces, and the walk actually did me some good. It cleared my head. Was eating that carton of ice cream a good decision? No. But it happened. I'm over it and I'm moving on.

After filling up Mr. MacDonald's water bowl with the hose, I walk to the screen door to let Mrs. MacDonald know I've returned.

Instead, there's a note on the door with my name on it.

Emma,

I had to run a very important errand. I currently have a plumber working in the house. Please stay in the kitchen and make sure nothing goes amiss. Make sure he doesn't swipe any crystal. Or any of my cross stitch pictures. The framed one above the dining room table is especially prized. Keep an eye on it.

Toodles,

Mrs. MacDonald

I don't get paid enough for this.

Walking into the kitchen, I find a pair of legs and work boots sticking out from underneath the sink. My entrance causes him to lift his head and bang it on a pipe. Water pours forth, drowning out the man's swearing.

"Oh no! I'm so sorry." I run over. "Are you okay?"

His hands work quickly while water pours over his shirt and jeans. I remove a yellow-and-white checkered tea towel from a drawer and toss it at him.

I stare at his face. This is not a fortyish, overweight man with the pair of saggy jeans that all plumber jokes are based around. Instead, a young Harrison Ford stands in front of me. Yum. His jeans fit *quite* nicely.

"Thanks," he says with a laugh, pushing himself up. "You scared me."

"I have that effect on people. Scaring them, I mean. I scare people. Boo!" I jab my hands in the air. *Shut up, Emma!*

"Duly noted."

He rubs the towel through his brown hair, but water remains in small beads on the tips. He looks at me with curiosity. Sweet heaven, his eyes are the kind of blue that is only possible through Photoshop.

"I'm Trevor." He extends his hand. I think about Ben in Mexico.

"Benny. I mean Emmy." I cough quickly and compose myself, tossing my hair. "Emma." I shake his hand. For a working man, his hands are soft. Someone knows the value of a good moisturizer. "Are you all done?"

"Almost." He points at the sink with his wrench. "Just a few more minutes."

He hands the tea towel back. I fold the cloth four times, then mash it into a ball. "Well, I guess I'll just hang out here and watch you until you're done."

I can't believe I just said that. Watch him until he's done? What is he going to think? I blush. Maybe I should go into the living room, sit on the couch with my head underneath a pillow, and contemplate my future as an ostrich. Fewer chances of embarrassing myself that way.

"Suit yourself," he says, sliding back under the sink. "Just don't get a drink of water from the tap yet."

I try not to stare.

Leaning against the counter, I can see our yard across the street. It looks pretty hilarious only half-mown. I should get on that.

Utter mess, that's me. Wasn't my heart broken and split apart just a few minutes ago? How is it that a cute plumber can make my armpits sweat and create visions of slow dancing in the rain? That's it. I'm swearing off Taylor Swift music. It's really not healthy for me.

"You know," Trevor says, standing up and closing the cabinet door beneath the sink, "there's one thing you should probably do if you plan on scaring anyone else today."

He takes a few steps towards me.

"Oh?"

"You might want to lose that cute ice cream moustache."

My eyes go wide and I clap my hand over my mouth. And yep, I can feel it—a sticky ice cream moustache above my upper lip. I want to die.

I grab a cloth and wipe my lip. "Well, there goes any chance of you kissing me."

The cloth falls from my hands as my brain registers the words that have left my mouth.

126

Trevor raises an eyebrow and a slow smile tugs at the corner of his lips.

What did I just say? What if he has a girlfriend? Worse, what if he's married? What if—

"I don't kiss on the first date," he says, holding my eyes.

I'm proud to say that I managed to twist a curl with my fingers and bite my lower lip before saying, "Duly noted."

————

Rash decisions are made by fools—and I'm a complete and utter fool.

Halfway into my burger and fries, I zone out but keep saying the customary "uh-huh" as Trevor drones on about the benefits of certain hubcaps over other hubcaps… something about hubcaps anyway.

I make a new decision, though. I'm taking the label off the ice cream carton and sticking it onto the grey painting in my room as a warning about what happens when I make decisions too quickly. First bad decision: jumping to conclusions over Facebook updates. Second bad decision: buying that litre of ice cream. Third bad decision: listening to my answering machine. Fourth bad decision: going out to dinner with Trevor.

Bad, bad, bad, bad.

"It all comes from trying to compete with Ben," I mutter.

"Who's Ben?"

"Uh, no one," I scramble. "I thought we were talking about cars. I meant Benz." I lean forward, feigning interest. "It all comes from competing with Benz and other foreign automakers."

Trevor sits back and finishes his milkshake with a slurp. "You know, Emma, you're smarter than you look."

I consider the decisions I've made today. "Not really."

Trevor breaks into a laugh. An annoying, irritating laugh. I need to wrap up my comedy routine or this is going to be a longer night than it already has been.

"Hey, you want another burger?" Trevor offers.

"No thanks."

"Okay, well, I'm going to get one."

Trevor and his annoying laugh leave the table, just as my phone buzzes.

It's Katie.

"I got your email, Katie," I say, bringing the phone to my ear. "Your place looks amazing."

"It's pretty cool, huh?"

Trevor's back is to me as he places his order.

"What are you doing?" Katie asks.

"You'll never guess. I'm on a date from h-e-double-hockey-sticks!"

Katie laughs with surprise. "You are not!"

"No, I'm serious. I'm on a date and it's horrible. He's talking about cars and he slurps his milkshake. And he said I was smart."

"That doesn't sound too bad."

"He said I was smarter than I looked."

"Ouch," Katie says, a hint of consolation in her tone. "Well, wait, what are you wearing?"

"Oh, shut it! Look, he's coming back. How do I get rid of him?"

"You really are on a date?"

"Yeah, yeah. Monumental moment. Now, tell me how to get rid of him." Katie's laughter fills my ears. Everyone's laugh sounds annoying today. "Katie, I'm serious, he's coming back."

"Oh, this is too funny."

"Some friend you are."

I shut the phone with force as Trevor returns to his seat.

His eyebrow raises. "Aggressive telemarketer?"

"No, just some crazy lady who's going to die alone and friendless."

"Oh. Was that the lady whose house I was just at?"

I burst out laughing. "Something like that." I stop laughing. Trevor is staring at me. "What?"

Trevor shrugs. "I like your laugh."

Our eyes meet. His gorgeous blue eyes are looking into mine. I think we even have the potential to share a moment, except that I can't help but think his eyes should be Ben's chocolate brown eyes instead.

Looking away, I study the napkin on the tray in front of me. How am I going to explain myself? I'm making bad decisions. Albeit no one has died as a result, but I'm being emotional, jumping at any chance to try and move on like Ben is doing so effortlessly.

"Trevor, listen, I had fun tonight... sort of, but..."

"Uh-oh, you're giving me the brush-off and it's not even dessert." He points to the two baked apple pie tarts.

Gosh, he *is* cute.

"It's the 'smarter than you look' comment, isn't it?" Trevor scratches the back of his head. "I knew it! I'm not really good at being smooth, as evidenced by my rambling monologue about cars. It's just that you have this..."

I may not want a future with Trevor, but I do want him to finish his sentence. I smile brightly.

"You... you just have this delicate beauty to you. You make me nervous. When I'm nervous, I talk about cars."

I have a delicate beauty. And then something else about cars. That's all I hear.

I bite my lip and make a promise to myself that I won't be swayed by a pair of jeans ever again.

Ever.

He stares at me with a softened expression. Maybe if things were different there would be a chance of something happening between us.

Then he laughs.

An irritating laugh.

Nope, not a chance in h-e-double-sticks.

I'm out the truck door before Trevor has even fully braked.

"Hey, Emma."

I turn around, but only to be polite. I'm a bit embarrassed by tonight's events.

He holds out a business card. "I would like you to have my number."

He has such an endearing look. I put him through a horror show of an evening, and still he pursues me.

"Thanks, Trevor." I even smile sweetly.

"You bet. Call that number if you ever need a plumber."

He waves and backs out of the driveway.

Walking towards the front steps in the fading blush of day, I sink to the ground. The cement is warm from the day's intense heat. The flowers are in full bloom, colourful and shiny.

A soft wind blows, making me think of whispers and promises. And Mexico. And tubs of ice cream.

"Jesus, I'm confused. I thought I was starting to heal. I made some progress in Montana. It certainly seemed that way in art class. But now I'm hurting all over again. Today has been an absolute gong show. A complete failure. Without realizing it, I was trying everything to rid my life of grey, but I can't do it in my own strength. I want my life to be a lush garden, not this grey mass of nothingness."

My Father is the Gardener.

"Lord, will you make my life a garden?"

Will you let me weed and prune?

I see a brown rock and pick it up. I weigh it in my hands, considering my options. "How about a xeriscape rock garden? I could use some low maintenance work here, God."

Silence.

"Don't you have some weeding to do in Mexico?"

Silence.

I long for the rich colours of a flower garden. Magenta, coral, scarlet. Sonya the Crazy Substitute Art Teacher says that we need to experience the depths of colour. I'm still haven't progressed much beyond grey, though. It'll take me forever to grow beautiful, won't it?

I am the Master Gardener.

"I suppose I could trust you to use pruning shears responsibly."

Every branch that bears fruit I prune so that it bears more fruit.

I shake my head and pocket the rock. I may have failed today and lived emotionally, but I'm adding this rock to my collection. This, too, is going to be part of my altar.

Chapter Twenty-Two

I was wearing a yellow dress when Ben first told me he loved me. I bet he wasn't even planning on telling me that day. It's not like him to let things "just happen." He's a planner, though if I said that he would correct me and say he was a strategist.

And I would stick my tongue out at him and say, "Perfectionist."

Nonetheless, the words "I love you" crossed his lips and surprised us both.

I had just finished chatting with an elderly woman while on a walk in the park one day. She wore a fuchsia sundress and a jewelled brooch. I remember thinking she was classy.

As I was walking away, the fabric of the skirt brushed against me. That dress had four layers, short pieces that grew longer at each tier. I was feminine and sweet.

I had sighed from contentment. It was one of those rare moments when you're fully present with no thoughts of the future and no shadows of the past.

"I love you, Emma."

I looked up at Ben, who stood a few feet from me. His shirt was rolled up to his elbows and his brown eyes seemed to caress my face. He was looking at me. Into me. I had an overwhelming sense that my life had always been progressing towards this moment, that each step I took, every dark road I travelled, had been about bringing me to this place.

Those precious words found their way inside me and opened doors to rooms of joy that had been locked, forgotten, sworn off.

My smile grew into a beaming grin. I moved forward to reach him and thought I heard bells.

And then I realized that I *did* hear bells. Bicycle bells. A cyclist was trying to warn us that he was about to pass. The cyclist breezed by and brought normalcy to our enchanted moment. Perhaps he grabbed the beauty of it as he sped off down the path. No matter how romantic I wanted my life to be, reality had a way of invading it.

Ben broke out into an easy grin.

He loved me.

Me!

I stepped forward and playfully tagged him on the arm. "You're it! You have to catch me."

I turned and ran up the small slope onto a grassy field. I could hear him behind me, laughing, trying to catch me but enjoying the chase.

My heart was full. I'd thrown back my head and let out a gleeful laugh.

I, Emma Carmichael, was being chased by love.

To this day, I love that yellow dress.

Looking over the desk in my spare bedroom, I'm impressed with myself. I've finally found the courage to throw away the wedding programs we made. That's $150 I'll never see again. I keep a few extra copies of the wedding invitations, too, but I toss the reply cards.

I have managed to file all the bills and contracts related to the wedding. I probably don't need them, but I'm loathe to throw away receipts until at least a year has passed. My dad ingrained that in me.

I manage to wrap up the yellow dress and put it in a box. I'm probably being dramatic, but that dress is special. Every time I wore it after that spring day, I wore it for Ben. I can't look at it hanging in the closet every day, but I can't give it away, either. There are some memories I don't want to forget, even though they're painful.

Now all I have left is a small pile in the middle of the floor: a heap of pretty things I planned to decorate the church with, a box of mints, and other odds and ends. I hope Mandy will take them off my hands for her own wedding.

I dial her number while wiping down the walls.

It wasn't supposed to be like this. Mandy and I had planned our weddings at the same time. We even tried on dresses together in Calgary. She bought the dress I tried on initially and I decided to order the one she wore first. We giggled over getting married and how proud Tammy would be of us. We've come a long way since our days together at the Girls Home.

The phone goes to voicemail as I pace the floor.

"Hey Mandy. It's me, Emma. I got your email. Sorry I've been so quiet." I consider making excuses, but Mandy knows me too well. "It's been a hard couple of months, but I'm starting to unthaw from the shock of it all. I haven't done a great job at being a friend and bridesmaid. I'll start making it up to you when I come to your wedding shower."

I say goodbye, then hang up.

I hope I can make amends for neglecting her. I also hope she doesn't pick that hideous green colour for our bridesmaid dresses.

Chapter Twenty-Three

"Dad said they're making repairs on rural churches in Nicaragua. And he's helped a few single moms create business plans."

Sunday dinner is in full swing. Gigi has made roasted corn and Papa and Uncle Fred barbecued hotdogs and hamburgers. It's a summer feast complete with potato and macaroni salads.

I look around the table and can hardly believe it's been a month since I was fired and blew up at everyone. I've come a long way. Today in particular has been full of fresh starts, including attending church with Natalie and Mark.

Holding up a glass, I clear my throat. "I just want to toast all of you. Last month I was a bit…" I pause to find the right word.

"Dramatic," Natalie suggests.

"Hysterical."

"Over the top."

"Weird."

My glass comes down to rest on the table. "I was going to say upset, but yes, your descriptions fit. Anyway, I was rude and I'm sorry. We all have our quirks. Whether it's my predictable outbursts," I make eye contact with Andrea, "or Mark's constant teasing or Uncle Fred pretending he's not smoking again, we all have them. Here's to our family."

Cheers go up around the table and glasses are hoisted in the air.

Gigi looks pointedly at Uncle Fred. "When did you start smoking again?"

Everyone at the table bursts out laughing, even Uncle Fred. Apparently, sweet Gigi is the only one who remained in the dark. She wags her finger at him.

Sometimes I just swell with love for our family dinners.

Amidst the chatter, the distinct sound of Andrea's phone goes off. She glances at her cell phone and then shoves it back onto her lap. Her fork plays with the potato salad, but she's not serious about eating anything. She sits for a few moments before getting up abruptly and leaving.

Papa nods in her direction. "Everything okay?"

Aunt Cindy brushes crumbs from her napkin. "Oh, Andrea's got a broken heart," she says dismissively, rolling her eyes. "Her boyfriend of two minutes broke up with her."

I cover my gasp by coughing. The potato salad sits heavy in my stomach.

"You know what it's like at this age." Aunt Cindy butters her corn. "She'll be fine. Andrea can work out her angst in those art classes of hers."

"And not spend all our money at the malls," Uncle Fred adds. He reaches for another hamburger as he tells us about his upcoming business trip to Vancouver.

I watch in horror as everyone resumes small talk. Doesn't anyone care about Andrea? Doesn't anyone realize how important her boyfriend was to her?

"Excuse me," I say quietly. Only Natalie notes my quick exodus. Sliding open the patio door, I step into the backyard.

I haven't been out here in a while. The twinkly lights are plugged in, even though the night sky hasn't yet made an appearance. It's so pretty. A perfect place for an outdoor wedding.

When I open my eyes, I spot Andrea tucked into the low arm of a birch tree. As I approach, her corduroy hat flies at me and I try to dodge it. No luck.

I look up and gasp. Hidden beneath Andrea's cap is bleach white hair. A girl breaks her heart and her hair takes the beating.

"Hey," Andrea says. It has all the welcome of a door being slammed in my face.

"Can I come up?"

Andrea shrugs. "If you want."

I struggle to get a foothold on the tree. I'm getting too old to climb trees. Andrea finally holds out her hand and helps me up.

"Thanks," I say, brushing the bark and small pieces of accumulated green lichen off my clothes. I take a deep breath. *God, please help me.*

Andrea's shoulders are slumped as she plucks leaves and rips them into small pieces. I can only think of one way to connect with Andrea, and I know it will be painful.

"The night Ben proposed to me, I wore Nina's pearl earrings."

Andrea stops fileting the leaf.

"She gave them to me the year I turned thirteen," I continue. "I'd never worn them until that day. I'd never *wanted* to wear them. I just kept them in a tiny grey box. Sometimes I would hold them up to my ears and look in the mirror to see what they looked like. I never put them on, though."

The setting sun brushes golden light across the Andrea's face. She listens intently.

"Nina told me that every woman needs a pair of pearl earrings. It was the most thoughtful gift she ever gave me. I was home for Christmas, as you know. Ben saw the earrings and asked me to wear them. He said that we were going to do something special, and wouldn't they look great? My resolve to never wear them wilted like Gigi's rose bush over there." Cool air ripples through the sad-looking bush with clinging pink petals. "I wore them for him. I thought that somehow choosing to love Ben more than the wounds my mother inflicted on me was a sign that I was worthy of being a special woman. Foolish, I know.

"Two days after Ben demolished my heart, I drove out of town and stopped by a river. I wanted to scream. Instead I threw away those pearl earrings. Two pearls, two people who had ripped my heart in two. I wanted the earrings to hit the bottom of the river and be buried in mud.

I half-hoped they would take my pain with them."

I tuck my hair behind my ear. Confessing that out loud isn't half-bad.

Andrea clears her throat. "I buried Rudy's goldfish in my backyard. The whole bowl and everything."

Apparently acting bizarrely when crushed is a family trait.

"I want him to be frustrated every time he goes, by habit, to feed the fish," Andrea says. "He'll miss it, you know. I want him to miss something that he had access to everyday. Kind of like me."

"That sounds normal to me, Andrea."

"Yeah, well... he already got a new fish."

"Ouch."

I reach over and grab her hand, a sign of solidarity. She doesn't pull away.

"Andrea." Gigi's soft voice carries out from the screen door and wraps us together like string around a brown paper package. "It's time to go."

Andrea squeezes my hand and then releases it.

"I can drive you home," I offer.

"Really?" She seems to weigh her options. "No, I should go with *them*." An acid tone drips on the final word. "Dad says I can drive."

I laugh. "Oh boy."

Andrea starts to climb down from the tree.

"Thanks, Emma." The silence is awkward, as though this is the first time Andrea has been so genuine with someone. "Thanks for listening and stuff."

Gigi's voice sounds again, only to be bulldozed by Aunt Cindy's shrill tone. She stretches Andrea's name into a three-syllable weapon of war.

"Stay between the ditches," I call to Andrea's disappearing back.

She sticks her fist up in the air and pumps it twice. "Beep, beep!"

Andrea and I have finally crossed a bridge in our relationship. With a few small gestures, our budding friendship could bloom. A few ideas come to me.

I stay up in the tree until the air is heavy and the sun starts to turn back its blankets and tuck itself into bed. The sound of cars starting and family leaving interrupts the emerging crickets.

I look around the garden and my throat tightens. Good things have happened in this place. Countless memories of finding hidden Easter eggs in the bushes, grabbing fallen branches to use as arms for newly made snowmen, sitting in the shade eating strawberries in juice-stained white shirts.

"Looks like the sunset is going to be a beaut." Papa approaches, rolling a rock in his hand.

"It does," I offer.

"How's our Andrea?"

"She's devastated, but she'll be okay."

"And how's our Emma?"

"Actually, Papa, it helped me to sit with Andrea. I talked to her about some of my recent heartache. It felt good to share it."

"Weep with those who weep. That sounds familiar," his deep voice rumbles. He studies the rock in his hand. "You're going to be just fine. Give it time, Emma. Give it time. Ben will come to his senses."

I don't think that will happen. "And if he doesn't?"

Papa reaches up while I extend my arm down to take the rock from him. "Then you will have come to yours."

Chapter Twenty-Four

Light pours in through the large open windows, bringing peace with it. The art studio is growing on me. I'm getting used to the smells of pastels and paints. Even our easel areas have a certain appeal.

Andrea is busy texting. I smile to myself. She has no idea what I have planned for her later today. My phone buzzes and I check the text: *Do you want to go to a matinee on Monday?*

I check the sender and laugh. Looking up at Andrea, I say, "I'm right here."

She shrugs and takes on the pose of an angel.

After this weekend's bonding session, I finally caved and decided to give Andrea my cell number. This is already her fifth text. I may come to regret this decision.

I text back: *No can do, amigo. Sorry. I have a date.*

My phone buzzes back in seconds. *With whom?*

I'm impressed. Andrea knows her grammar.

For a brief moment, I remember my horrible date with Trevor. I'll have to tell Andrea about it and warn her not to go out on any rebound dates.

I type back: *None of your beeswax.*

She doesn't need to know that I'm meeting with Tammy.

Monique walks in front of the class and claps her hands. She's wearing a peasant blouse and jean skirt. And I love her chunky-heeled shoes.

"Today we'll begin to create layers on our canvases. The idea is to cover things up, then peel portions back. We're going to look at different ways to add depth and dimension to our individual pieces." Monique reaches over and grabs her coffee cup, tilting her head to the side with a philosophical expression. "Our lives are rich with layers. Our journey is often about building on what we already know. We, as human beings, are like great masterpieces of layers. Layers of emotions, experiences, thoughts, belief, passion, and ideas."

Her eyes rove around the room as she sips from her mug. I hold my breath, hoping she won't lead us in a deep meditation or force us to hum.

"Let's dig deep and explore those layers. An exercise, if you will." She reaches over to the table and pulls up a piece of used wrapping paper. "We're going to repurpose this piece of paper. We're going to breathe fresh life into something that has become diminished and purposeless. Tell me, what does this piece of paper represent, besides wrapping paper?"

"Well, it's blue," Andrea offers. "It makes me think of a calm lake." She looks back at me and crosses her eyes. She's just trying to be cheeky, but Monique ponders it.

"Okay." Monique nods, making her hoop earrings swing back and forth. "Let's dig deeper. Who's looking at this calm lake? Why are they there?"

"Because they're stressed," Clarke says.

"Okay." She puckers her lips. "Why?"

The room is silent. Even the guy who normally chews gum—and then incorporates it into each painting—is still.

"Come on, class. Layers. Why are they stressed?"

"They have no money," the gum-chewer says.

"Why?"

"Their house burned down," someone else volunteers.

"How?"

Andrea shrugs. "They left a candle burning."

Monique paces the aisle with her gaze fixed on me. "Why were they using a candle, Emma?"

I gulp, searching my imagination. "It was an anniversary in their life and they wanted to remember it. But they forgot to blow the candle out, so it actually destroyed a safe place for them."

The blue piece of wrapping paper is lifted high into the air. Monique paces, holding up her trophy. "Do you see the layers contained in this colour? It isn't just blue, is it?"

Our class murmurs recognition.

"This paper tells a story. Your job, as an artist, is to tell stories. But don't let them be one-dimensional tales. Tell a *whole* story. Whisper the secrets of the background. Weave together the details of the past and the present to create a work that speaks to the observer. The best stories are rooted in layers that emerge slowly, revealing truth."

This is why people become artists. What she's saying resonates deep within me. I look around the room and see every article available to me with fresh eyes. What story am I going to tell? Where will I begin?

"I really got into this whole layers thing!" Andrea wiggles in her seat from excitement. "Isn't Monique the most inspiring person ever?"

Will this be another anime drawing depicting a battle between good and evil, perhaps involving flying monkeys and guys with green hair?

"I decided to tackle my inner angst," she says, pointing to the messy pile of scrap paper cluttering her workspace

Oh boy.

I aim to prepare a compliment ahead of time, in case her piece ends up being black paper covered in black nail polish followed by a paper goldfish shellacked in tissue paper.

Andrea presents her piece to me with a flourish. The browns, reds, and blacks collide behind ticket stubs and soda labels. The items on top have been stained with teabags, lending everything a sepia tone.

"Wow. It looks very…"

"Angry, right?" Andrea points to the ticket stub. "I'll explain my story. The stripe of black over the ticket stub represents this memory I have."

I move in closer.

"My mom promised she would take me to a play. I got all dressed up and waited. And waited. And waited. Finally, she called and said she couldn't make it because of some work crisis."

"Are you going to show the piece to your mom?"

"She won't care if I do."

I open my mouth to give some advice. Then I close it. I've just started to establish a connection with Andrea. I'll have to be patient if she's going to trust me enough to let me speak into her life.

"What about you?" Andrea walks back to my canvas and shrieks. "Please tell me you have more than this! Another completely grey canvas?"

I can't blame her. It *is* pathetic. Even the gum-chewer has found a way to use his gum wrappers in a unique way.

I point to all the things I've gathered. "Grey is just the beginning. It's the background. I'm going to add all these elements to the page."

Andrea sifts through the pile of papers, strings, magazines, and shopping bags in front of me. She pushes aside the rolls of wrapping paper and accidentally sends the fabric scrap bag flopping onto the floor. Reaching into a box full of seashells, she holds up a child's sandal. "Seriously?"

"I was hoping it would represent taking a new step in life."

"How were you going to get this onto the canvas? With crazy glue?"

I stick my nose up, offended. "Maybe."

Andrea tosses the shoe back. She looks at my accumulated pile. "Emma, you can't create a story on canvas with this much junk. It clutters up the meaning. Stories are always simple. What makes them complex are the details."

Where was I when Andrea grew an intellect? How long has this been going on without my knowledge? "You are totally right."

Andrea gives a smug look. "I know."

I roll my eyes. "Okay, so what do I do?"

"Pick three items to start, then move this junk out of here."

———

"Here you go!"

I've been waiting for this moment all day, so much so that I hardly hear a word Dr. Martha says as I drive around town. I asked Aunt Cindy if I could spend the rest of the day with Andrea and forego our typical parking lot drama. What Andrea needs most right now is one-on-one girl time. There's no better cure for a broken heart.

"Ah!" Andrea shrieks as I pull into her favourite fast food restaurant. "How did you know I love their chili cheese dogs?"

"You said something about them once at Gigi and Papa's. You claimed they were the ultimate comfort food."

"I can't believe you remember that!"

"I do."

A few minutes later, we're pulling back onto the street. Andrea is already half-finished her cheese dog.

"I may not be your best friend," I say as she inhales the remaining bites, "but I do know how to eat sour candies, roll down the windows, and crank up the music."

It was only a few weeks ago that Andrea confided this secret dream to me. Is it still important to her? Out of the corner of my eye, it's clear. She's beaming.

"And Chinese fire drill?"

I roll my eyes dramatically. "Okay, if we have to!" I point to the glove compartment. "I think you'll find a tub of sour candy in there, missy."

"Thank you!" Andrea retrieves the candy and dives into it with panache.

We stop at a red light behind a blue pickup truck.

"Chinese fire drill!" I shout, putting the car in park. Shoving my door open, I race around the car. Andrea giggles as we pass each other at the front of the car.

Honk!

My eyes grow wide. The light is green already and I'm only at Andrea's side door.

"Get in!" Andrea yells.

"No way! You aren't driving my car."

Honk, honk!

A guy leans out his window and yells something.

"Calm down, this isn't Calgary!" Andrea shouts back.

Dear God, please let Andrea know how to drive. Please don't let me die. Please.

Andrea gets behind the wheel. After a few blocks, I'm still too busy pleading for my life and gripping the door handle to realize that Andrea is managing rather well.

She grins at me, unaware that she has a chili stain on her chin. She looks adorable. Why did I ever find her annoying?

"Well, looks like I just showed everyone who the better cousin is," she says.

Oh, yes. That's why.

Andrea cranks up the music. I'm about to join her in song when I my mouth opens wide.

"Stop!"

Andrea slams on the brakes. With wide eyes, she looks every which way to see if we were about to collide with something.

A horn sounds behind us.

I'm frozen in shock as Andrea puts the signal light on, checks her mirrors, and peers over her shoulder.

"I'm pulling over," Andrea says.

Pull over. Roll over. Fall over and faint. I don't care what she does. I just want to evaporate and forget the horror I'm witnessing.

Andrea parks the car. "Emma, what the hell was that about? We could have had an accident if that guy behind us was following too closely."

I manage to point towards the side of the road.

"What? All I see are two kids skateboarding and an old man going into the flower store."

My voice comes out shallow and scratchy. "Beside him."

"What? The store? The Blushing Bride? What about it?"

"The window."

In the picture window, framed by a display of tulle and suspended flowers, is my wedding dress. A simple white, full A-line skirt with a sequenced bodice and a lace-up back.

"Wow! Look at that dress. It's gorgeous."

I hiccup.

We sit in stunned silence. That's the effect the dress has, the power it holds. It renders you speechless.

I was speechless the first time I saw it on Mandy. It was so beautiful that it required a Selah-type moment to fully comprehend its simple extravagance. I was doing cartwheels in my head when Mandy said she didn't think it was the gown for her. I slipped it on and stood in the dressing room, having a quiet moment to myself before coming out to show Katie, Mandy, and her cousin. I remember swaying in that dress. It made the most glorious sound. When I looked in the mirror, I knew: this was *the dress*. This gown would be the fabric that held together the memories of my new life with Ben. This dress would carry me like a cocoon and be the chamber of my transition from Emma Carmichael to Mrs. Benjamin Fenton.

But it never had a chance to bring about the promised metamorphosis.

My body is numb. Is this what post-traumatic stress feels like? Seeing the dress is a definite trigger, and now this is the part where I fall apart. Andrea will drive me to the hospital, where they'll relax me with drugs until I can undergo a psych evaluation. The nurse will offer me green jello.

I suck in a breath and wait to fall apart.

Nothing happens.

I hold my breath, worried that my shock will turn to panic. Panic will turn to tears. Tears will turn to country music.

Still nothing.

I conjure up the memory of returning that wedding dress to the store. I had ordered it locally, for the sake of convenience. There was no convenience to be found in being denied a full refund, though. It was a horrible experience. Nothing hurt more than parting with that dress.

You know, besides the whole broken heart, losing the man I love part.

But losing the dress came a close second. Losing my dignity took the bronze.

Andrea looks at me, then at the window display. "*That* was your dress?"

My response is soft. "It was."

"It's stunning."

Andrea and I sit staring at the dress.

"Want a sour candy?"

"Yeah."

We eat the whole tub in silence. Later, I have a stomach ache.

Chapter Twenty-Five

"**A**re you excited?"

Inside the Calgary Tower restaurant, Mandy is finishing the last bite of cheesecake on her plate. We both agree that it's only right—noble, really—for us to eat cheesecake after our shopping expedition. Perusing the markets can take a lot out of a girl, and cheesecake can put it all back in.

"I'm so excited, Emma," Mandy says while playing with one of the three hoops in her right ear. "It's starting to feel real. All the months of wedding planning and shopping are behind me. Now it's my wedding shower. Next, I'll be getting married!"

"I can't believe it's a week away. The time passed so quickly." I sip my water. I've assured Mandy three times already that I'm happy to be here and want to hear all about her wedding. "Tell me about the shower today."

Mandy raises her eyebrows. "Debra planned it."

If I had water in my mouth, it would have come spitting back out. "What? Please tell me you're joking!"

"I wish I was."

Debra is like a boa constrictor. She has this way of inviting herself to everything. She then weaves herself around a project in such a way that you feel warm and contented about it—until she squeezes every remaining ounce of strength out of you.

I put on my best supportive bridesmaid face. "How wonderful! I'm sure every detail is in hand. It will be a great shower."

Mandy moans. "She picked her favourite colours to decorate, Emma."

I wipe my mouth with the cloth napkin. "That's good. Different. You don't want to overdo your wedding colours, or we'll all be bored of them by next Saturday."

"Em, she ignored my requests for a retro, vintage-style party. She's turned it into a fiesta feast."

I sip my water, buying myself time to think up a positive response.

"It's Mexican-themed!"

I swallow an ice cube.

Mandy shakes her head. "Doesn't she know that bridal showers and beans don't mix?"

I start to laugh.

"What's so funny?"

"Maybe I'm becoming callous to your plight, Mandy. I like to think that after the past three months of not being married, I've learned at least one thing: don't make a big deal out of the lead-up to the wedding. I think of all the hours I wasted worrying over deejays and centrepieces. The only thing I should have been worrying about was the one thing I never gave a moment's thought to."

"You're right. It's not that big a deal. Now, are you sure you're going to be okay, Emma? You don't have to come. You can watch a movie back at my apartment and we'll meet up for sushi afterwards like we planned, okay?"

"Stop asking me that. I'm here for you. Besides, I owe you. If I hadn't been so checked-out lately, I would have thrown you that über-chic vintage party you asked for and Debra might not have taken over."

We look at each other and burst out laughing.

Neither one of us believe that. Not with Hurricane Debra around.

———

Mexican music oozes out the windows of Mandy's two-story childhood home. I poke her in the ribs and try to get her to salsa dance up the stairs. She points at the sombreros turned upside-down and made into makeshift flower pots. The geraniums and orange pansies are an interesting mix.

So is the green and brown spike of a bullrush.

"It's going to be fine," I say, consoling Mandy. "Remember, you gave Debra the wedding shower so she wouldn't touch your reception plans."

"I know. It's like she's taking her revenge on me."

I laugh. "No, remember this is Debra. Her tastes are…"

"Abominable."

"I was going to say eclectic."

"You are too nice, Emma."

"Not really. It's just that I've had my own experiences with poorly behaving cousins lately."

The front door holds a bright orange posterboard declaring "Fiesta at Casa de Boersma." I take a picture of Mandy with my phone. She poses with a thumbs-up and exaggerated wink.

Just then, a trio of women throw open the door, screaming with enthusiasm.

Mandy tried to warn me at the restaurant that her cousins were excited about her wedding. I just didn't realize that excited meant psycho.

The gaggle of cousins leads Mandy into the living room. I take off my shoes and follow, where a woman dressed in a lime green wrinkle skirt and matching tanktop twirls around.

"Isn't it wild?" the woman asks.

I stuff a chip in my mouth to spare me from commenting. The room is full of red and orange streamers. A giant donkey piñata hangs from the ceiling and brightly coloured Mexican blankets rest on every available chair. Placed around the living room are various rooster statues and dried pepper wreaths.

Plastering on a smile, I look for three highlights to point out to Mandy later. First, twinkly lights. Second, candles (I'll generously leave out the fact that the candle holders are tacky). And finally, the food; this I found no fault with, since it's all Mexican. Tamales, burritos, tacos.

But tacos at a wedding shower? I bought a new blouse for this party. I'm not wearing meat and cheese on my clothes, and we all know that's what happens when you eat tacos in public.

I sit on a chair draped in a sash that reads "Ole." Debra spared no expense. Cousins!

I pull out my phone, snap a picture, and text Andrea. I wish she was with me. I think we would have found a lot of inspiration in this place. We could have pocketed the remains of the piñata to repurpose for art class.

"You can put your gift for the bride here," the green-clad woman says, pointing a red fingernail at the table. Mandy introduces us and I find out this is Debra's mother. For some reason, I'm not surprised.

I deposit my gift and take in the ambiance, wondering if this is anything close to what Mexico is really like.

My heart lurches. Ben is in Mexico... or at least he was. Maybe he still is.

I take a calming breath. I don't need to think about Ben right now. Not at a wedding shower.

Thoughts of my own wedding shower spring to mind. Natalie and Katie had planned it. It was an elegant tea. Gigi whispered the secrets to a great marriage. Aunt Cindy asked if Papa had made the punch before drinking it. Andrea texted the whole time. Katie and Natalie did a ridiculous poem reading. Mandy pranked me with a pair of old granny panties to wear on my honeymoon; Gigi ended up taking them home.

Taking a deep breath, I resolve not to think about Ben. Today is about Mandy, not me. I'm not going to get worked up.

I won't cry, either. And if I do, I'll blame it on the jalapenos.

Chapter Twenty-Six

Debra claps her hands to settle the group. Cameras flash for a few minutes as the other women take pictures of Mandy wearing a giant sombrero. She smiles, flaunting the ridiculous hat.

The group then settles down and takes their seats. At the punch table, I ladle two glasses—one for me and the other for a woman sitting beside me. She receives it with thanks.

"Everyone in this room is here because of my amazing cousin, Mandy," Debra begins, squeezing Mandy's hand. Debra can be over the top in a very odd way, but she obviously loves her family. "We are here to celebrate someone who is unique, funny, gorgeous, and can't bake to save her life."

The group chuckles and a few catcalls come from women offering to take their gifts back. Mandy just wags her finger at Debra and says, "Hey! Be nice!" She blushes and looks every bit the happy bride-to-be.

"As most of you know, Greg proposed to Mandy in a very crazy way," Debra says once everyone is quiet again.

Debra's mother says, "Who ever heard of rigging a pinball machine to spell out 'Marry Me, Mandy' once she hit ten thousand points? You and your arcade games!"

Mandy beams. "And I told him my answer would be yes if he let me beat him at a game of air hockey. I won, ten to nothing!"

Debra claps at the silly story. "Since introductions need to be made, I thought each of us could share a unique and memorable engagement story. It can be your own or someone else's."

A murmur of excitement goes through the room. My breath is still and I stare at the bright piñata just behind Debra's head. Maybe I can break it open and knock her unconscious with jelly beans and gumdrops.

My insides roll, and it's not from the guacamole. This has to be the worst way to introduce oneself.

A woman named Laura recounts how her husband brought her to a fancy restaurant. He played a song he wrote on the guitar and then got down on one knee. "It was magical," she says, a wistful smile reaching her beautiful blue eyes. "Of course I said yes."

A collective sigh goes up from the group.

"That's a hard act to follow," a stout brunette says playfully. Everyone giggles and nods. "My Jim looked at me and said, 'My dad is giving me a piece of land to farm and raise a family on. What do you think about that?'"

I try to join in on the camaraderie, but my palms are sweaty and my throat may close up. I told Mandy that I could be here for her, but now I have serious doubts. The next person starts to tell their story, but my mind keeps pulling me back to my own.

The room seems to fade away and suddenly I'm in my own head—rather, I'm outside watching the frosty air turn my breath into white clouds. Light snow is falling onto the red woollen mittens Gigi made for me. The candle I'm holding in a tin can lantern is blooming and full. The wax is ripe and ready to spill over the edge in a liquid stream.

This was Christmas Eve, the night that changed my life forever.

We're finishing our neighbourhood carolling. The final bars of "The First Noel" fade away and Andrea and Jack run ahead of the group, claiming they have to get inside before they die from the cold. Somehow we get them to come back and join us for "Silent Night," which we always save for last.

Our final stop is Gigi and Papa's house. Usually Papa comes with us, but he stayed home this year for the first time ever, complaining of the cold and his knees. I miss his deep baritone voice.

Ben stands beside me, our bodies close enough to touch. Natalie and Mark ask Jack to ring the doorbell for Gigi and Papa while Uncle Fred and Andrea start up a snowball fight. Aunt Cindy, rambling on to my dad about something, sidesteps a spray of snow. Our tin can lanterns eke out just enough light to set a rosy glow on our faces.

Gigi and Papa open the door. The snowball hijinks end and everyone holds onto their lanterns once again. Dad starts the opening refrains of "Silent Night." We join our voices and began to sing the familiar melody. Gigi and Papa pull their winter coats tight and step out onto the porch, closing the door behind them. I smile to myself and wonder if they discussed all the heat they'd lose if they kept the door open.

I peek over at Ben. He looks adorable. His hat is pulled down to his eyebrows, snowflakes caught on his eyelashes. He catches my eye and I suck in a breath, forgetting the words temporarily. His eyes are so tender that I'm certain I can stay rooted to this spot, staring into them long past the candle's endurance.

We are a merry bunch, each of our noses and cheeks a robust red. Soon we come to the end: "Sleep in heavenly peace, sleep in heavenly peace..."

Love is in the air. Love is here. I thank Christ for coming to earth, for clothing Himself in skin and becoming a man acquainted with sorrow for my sake.

Love is here.

The final notes hang in the air. The snow falls quietly, the hush of holy reverence settling among us. I close my eyes to savour the moment.

"I thought we were going to be getting hot cocoa," Jack's voice calls out.

The group laughs and Papa opens the door to let everyone in.

Ben tugs me back to himself while Andrea and Jack scoot inside. Natalie's voice can be heard above the shuffling feet: "Joyeux Noel, Gigi." Mark adds, "Feliz Navidad."

Andrea holds the door open and gestures for us to come in. "Come on in, slowpokes."

My dad exchanges a look with Ben. "Ben and Emma will be in soon enough."

I suspect nothing. With my mittens on, my hands feel safe and warm tucked inside Ben's hand. I wrap my arms around him and sigh. This is my safe place.

I linger in the moment, fully capturing the essence of this night. It needs to be imprinted on my consciousness—the snowflakes falling, the chilled air, the shine of the candlelight casting shadows on the snow.

Ben steps back, grinning at me in such a silly way. It makes me think he might be waiting to dump snow down my back… just to hear me scream.

He clears his throat, and suddenly is as serious as I've ever seen him. He removes a leather glove, caressing my face. His hand lingers over my pearl earrings—the ones Nina gave me—as he says, "You are so beautiful, Emma."

Tears fill my eyes and my knees turn weak. I could spend forever with eyes like his looking into mine. His brown eyes are a mix of intensity and desire. They almost frighten me. They make me feel… like a woman. I blush.

"Emma, I want you with me always."

I can only nod.

"You are the most amazing person I have ever known." He looks up at the sky, struggling, it seems, to put his thoughts into words. That's unusual for him. I lean forward and put my red mitten against his mouth.

"Shhh!"

Part of me can't hear what he's about to say. If Ben is going to talk about how lovely and beautiful I am, I'll believe it. I want to be the embodiment of those words for him. I'm still getting used to the idea of being loved.

Ben shakes his head and frowns. I watch his neck and jaw. Oh Lord, he drives me wild.

"I have to say this, Emma. You have to listen to me."

I nod, a small smile on my lips.

"I love you. I want you." He lowers his voice. "I need you."

I'm going to faint, but Ben's hand steadies me. He chuckles to himself. "I can't believe I'm doing such a terrible job of this."

I stare back at him, my heart starting to beat a little faster. "At what?"

154

"Emma, I want you with me. Always."

"I know. You just said that."

He tugs me towards the end of the porch. We take a few steps, then stop. "I want you by my side. I want to walk with you through life. I want you with me, no matter what comes around the corner."

He looks at me as though that's supposed to be a hint.

My eyebrows come together in question and I tilt my head. "Around the corner?"

Ben grins. "Yep. No matter what lies around the corner."

My eyes go wide. Something *is* around the corner—around the corner of the porch. Taking two steps, I round the corner and then lose the ability to breathe.

In the snow are dozens of tea light candles, forming the message, "Emma, will you marry me?"

I run towards these candlelit words with the joy of a child on Christmas morning. Is this for real? The words are literally burning themselves into my memory. I glance back at Ben.

He's right behind me. On one knee. His arm is stretched out, and in his hand he holds a black box.

The coveted black box!

I'm going to faint. I'm going to cry. I'm going to have to open the box so I can do both.

Ben's hand lifts the lid.

I start crying as I catch the glint of three emeralds. Tears course down my face as Ben explains the significance of each one. "Emeralds, as you know, are your birthstone. This one," he points to the first one, "is for the month we met."

I nod at the memory.

"This one," he points to the emerald in the middle, "is for the day when you wore the yellow dress."

"I love you, too, Ben." I manage between tears, remembering his admission that day.

"And this one," he says, pointing to the third emerald, "is for the month I'd like to marry you and be with you forever. This one is for our future."

I stare at the ring as he slips it on my finger.

"Be with me, Emma," Ben's rich voice asks. "Be with me always. Will you marry me?"

My mouth goes dry. I'm not certain I can draw breath. Love for this man is suffocating me and I'm not sure what to do.

I cry. I nod. I find my voice long enough to say, "Oh yes, Ben." My hands clasp to my chest. "Yes."

He comes to his feet and hugs me, picking me up and twirling me around.

Suddenly a raucous of noise erupts from the house. Crammed into every available spot in Papa's office window stands my cheering family. They're shouting, giving thumbs-up and high-fives. Papa salutes Ben and I realized who lit the candles while we were out carolling. My eyes fill with tears as everyone bangs on the window, whistling their approval.

I hug Ben. He holds me so tight I think fear will never wrap itself around me again.

Except fear *does* cloak me, as I realize I'm not standing on that wintery porch; I'm sitting in Mandy's living room. Terror and dread are like matching gloves covering my arms, making them feel dead heavy. I'll soon be next to speak. What will I say? *What will I say?*

I look around the room and spy redemption in my hand. With measured movements, I bring the cup of punch to my lips and intentionally pour the drink onto my clothes.

New blouse, shmew blouse. Desperate times call for desperate measures.

The liquid dribbles down my shirt, across my skirt, and onto the head of a small, yappy dog at my feet.

Score.

I excuse myself and run for the nearest bathroom.

Chapter Twenty-Seven

"Do you really think sushi and Mexican food is a good mix?" I ask Mandy, because I'm having serious doubts. I've never tried sushi before.

"Emma, it'll be fine." Mandy pulls the restaurant door open. "Greg and I go here all the time. I want you to see it. Besides, this is Japanese cuisine, not just sushi."

Still… beans followed by raw fish. I just can't wrap my head around that. Or my mouth.

We're seated quickly inside the swanky restaurant. The lights are dim and the decor is streamlined and simple: cherry blossom branches in sleek rectangular vases stand like guards before the dining area. The atmosphere is energetic and upscale.

"This is a really cool place, Mandy. But after this afternoon, I'm not going to eat anything suspect. My stomach can't handle it. I'm full up on Kleenex."

"Emma, we can leave if you want to. Or just grab something to-go and take it back to my place."

"It's fine, Mandy. Yes, I snotted my brains out in that bathroom, but it's kind of part of the process. Healing is hard. You know that."

Mandy stares at a scar on the inside of her wrist, artfully hidden in the white lily tattoo. "Yeah, it is." Her brown eyes meet mine. "Thanks for being here today, and for staying even through the hard parts."

I try to think of something else to talk about. I don't want to cry here, too. I've decided to go on a Kleenex fast.

"Emma, tell me the truth. Can you handle being a bridesmaid?"

I study the menu and pretend that I know what the word *nori* means.

"Listen, Em, you and I go way back. We've walked with each other through some of the darkest times of our lives. I was there the day you decided to give up cutting for good. And for all the choices that followed that decision." She succumbs to the habit of fidgeting with her earring. "I know that when everything went south with Ben, you told me you were going underground for a while. You needed space. And I get that. But, Em, I would have been there for you. Just like before. I'm here now. Don't put on a brave display for me. If you can't be my bridesmaid, just say so. It won't change anything between us."

I've thought about backing out. I'm not proud of it, but it has crossed my mind. Several times.

"Mandy, one day I'll be over Ben and life won't seem so… grey. When I look back on this time in my life, I want to know that I said no to the right things for the right reasons. I can't say no to being your bridesmaid. Will it be hard for me to be in the wedding? Probably. Will it be hard to do the right thing for you? Maybe. But you're worth it."

Mandy coughs. That's as close as she gets to crying.

The waitress sets down two bowls of miso soup and takes our orders. Her kimono glows blue under the subdued dining room lights. She bows before leaving the table, and I bob my head up and down in response.

"Thank you, Emma. That means a lot to me." Mandy smiles sadly, then fiddles with her napkin. "You aren't mad at me for introducing you to Ben, are you?"

"No," I say without needing to think about it. "Ben and I were supposed to meet. It had God's handiwork written all over it. I used to doubt that. I used to think God could have prevented my heart from breaking."

"But you don't anymore?"

"To say that God led me to a relationship with Ben, confirming to me several times in prayer to continue pursuing that relationship, only for God to change His mind at the last second, is to say that God doesn't value my heart. Or Ben's heart, for that matter. And that's not true. God deeply values my heart."

"So what do you think it is?"

I shrug. If I had the answer, I wouldn't be eating Kleenex boxes instead of burritos.

An idea bubbles to the surface of my mind. "Maybe we made a mistake. Maybe at some point, I stopped checking in with God to see if this was really His plan for me. Maybe Ben just made a huge mistake and he's embarrassed to own up to it. I don't know, Mandy. I try not to answer the 'why' question anymore. It's exhausting."

"So you've forgiven him?"

I take a deep breath and slowly exhale. "Yep."

Every day, every time I see the colour yellow I forgive him. Or turn on my non-existent air conditioning. Or think of my engagement ring locked in my dad's safe, sealed in an envelope with instructions not to open it until a year goes by.

"I have forgiven him," I say again. "And continue to forgive him whenever I need to."

"That takes a lot of grace, Emma. I'm proud of you."

"Don't be. Katie and I turned one of his photos into a dartboard after the breakup. I haven't thrown it away yet."

We begin to reminisce about the time we drew moustaches on all the photos on Tammy's bulletin board at the Girls Home.

"She made us write to each person and ask for a new picture. Do you remember that?" Mandy shakes her head from laughing so hard.

"I totally forgot."

Our waitress arrives with our food and places a tray of green-covered circular rice thingies. She bows before leaving and I bob my head again.

"These are called vegetable rolls, Em. It's a great introduction to eating sushi, as there's no raw fish in it. Just avocado and cucumber. Try one. Just think fresh and healthy."

Mandy launches into a mini spiel about the long Japanese tradition of eating sushi. She even cites some statistics about their country's heart disease rate. Apparently it's very low.

"You ready?" Mandy asks. "We'll both have one."

I watch as she removes the wooden chopsticks from their paper package. She rubs them together back and forth. I follow suit, feeling like a suave adult.

Biting my lip, I try to manoeuvre the chopsticks in my hand. Mandy encourages me, as though she's coaching a salmon to swim upstream. "You can do it."

Shakily, I get the sushi into my mouth—the whole piece at once, as Mandy instructed. I hope the chef is watching. I won't insult him with a half-bite.

Mandy watches me intently as I start to chew.

I gulp down the roll. "I think I'm going to be sick."

"What?" Mandy leans forward. "Is it the food?"

"No," I say, wincing. "It's my mother."

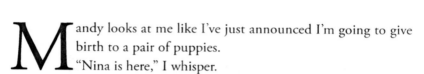

Chapter Twenty-Eight

Mandy looks at me like I've just announced I'm going to give birth to a pair of puppies.

"Nina is here," I whisper.

Mandy's eyes widen. "Where?" She leans forward on the table, craning her neck for a view.

"Over there. The booth with the man in the grey sweater."

As Mandy looks at Nina, I wonder if all she sees is the chic blond bob in the grey Armani suit. Does she see her for what she really is?

"That's your mom?"

"Mother," I correct her. I feel myself shrinking and wonder how many steps it is to the bathroom. "Yeah. That's her."

"Are you sure?"

"I think I know my own mother, Mandy."

Silence.

"But your mother abandoned you, didn't she?"

"Yeah."

"Well, she doesn't look like a wino. I mean, I thought she was an alcoholic bag lady who frequented shelters."

"What? Where did you get that idea?"

Mandy gives a slight laugh. "I pictured someone different. That woman over there doesn't look like the type of woman to leave her family. After all the stunts she pulled on you and Natalie, I figured she would have started drinking to curtail the guilt."

I glance to where Nina is sitting. "I wonder if that's her husband?"

"She's married?"

"Yep. He provides the money. She supplies the entertainment."

"Oh."

Well, really. What could Mandy say to that?

"She's looking over here, Emma."

I catch Nina's eyes and hold them for more than a second. Her eyes widen with recognition. Turning back to her husband, she flicks her arm in a dismissive gesture.

"Did she just…"

Ignore me? Reject me? "Yes, Mandy, she did."

———

This bathroom stall has nine large ceramic tiles. I've counted them four times already. They're grey granite and can hide dirt very well.

I think about the grey painting hanging on my bedroom wall. I make a mental note to grab a business card for this place on the way out. I'm going to staple it to that painting at home.

"All right," a voice calls from outside the bathroom. "Come out here. I know you're in there."

Nina.

Those are the same words she used when I was hiding in the pantry eating fistfuls of butter. I was five.

I stand up slowly and breathe in. *Help me, Jesus. Protect my heart. I can't take any more heartbreak today.*

I turn the round lock and watch the mechanism pull back into itself. I shyly pull the door open. I wish I could come across as defiant and proud. Factoring in the day I've had, I'm more like a lamb led to slaughter.

"Hi." I snap my head to the door and calculate a possible escape.

She runs a manicured hand over her smooth hair and brushes past me to stand in front of the mirror. After checking herself over, she turns to face me, her hands clasped in front of her.

"Hello, Chelsea."

"Nina."

I study the grey floor. I know that sounds weak, and I'm sure it is. The truth is that I'm still—still!—holding out hope that she'll come over and wrap her arms around me. My current dream is that I'll sob into her lapel and tell her all about the horrible, emotional day I've had—and she won't even mention that I've stained her jacket.

She unfolds her hands and fiddles with an earring. "They have great sushi here, don't you think?"

My eyes narrow. I haven't seen her in three years and she wants to talk about the sushi?

I clear my throat. "They have grey ceramic floors in here."

She looks at her feet. "Good choice. It hides the dirt well."

It almost sounds like we're talking code.

"What are you doing in Calgary, Nina?"

She looks at me in surprise. "I live here now."

"Mother!" Yes, I dropped the "m" word. Feel your age, lady! "How could you move back to Alberta and not let Nat and I know? Do you think Aunt Cindy likes being a go-between for you and everyone else? We're your daughters. You could at least let us know when something significant happens, like moving… or surgery."

I watch her flawless brow wrinkle like creased pants.

I snap my fingers. "Oh, I know why. Because you don't care. You don't care about anyone but yourself."

Nina picks at some imaginary lint on her suit. "Are you quite finished?"

I'm gearing up for round two when the door creaks open. The familiar kimono-wearing waitress sways into the room. "Is one of you named Emma?"

"Yes. That's me."

Nina turns to me in surprise. "Please tell me you're not still going by that ridiculous name."

I ignore her. I've been going by Emma for six years now. If she can't keep up, I'm not going to slow down to get her up to speed. That's what Facebook is for.

"This is for you." The waitress hands me a napkin. I grab it from her and bow. This is turning into a gong show.

I unfold the napkin:

Meet you at the front. –M."

Mandy. Thy name is salvation.

I brush past my mother. Pushing the door open, I walk through the dining room, head held high. I'm not going to lie. It feels good to be the one walking out this time.

Mandy is waiting by the entrance, eyes fixed on the bathroom door as I come out.

"I may have to nominate you for Friend of the Year," I say, passing her and heading outside. Before I do, I grab a business card from the counter.

"Katie will be crushed." Mandy pockets the receipt from dinner.

If life followed my script, my mother would come chasing after me. But I'm putting distance between us with every step I take. I can't stand here and wait for the impossible to happen.

Nina, Ben, ice cream that won't cause weight gain… none of it is going to happen.

I'm done waiting, God. I just want to walk away.

Mandy walks behind me, following at a slower pace. I march down the streets I passed an hour ago when we first drove to the restaurant. They seemed so droll and full of charm then. Now they seem garish and carnival-like.

When I judge that I've gone far enough, I sink onto a nearby bench like a stone dropped into water. Life flows around me—people walk, cars drive past—but through it all, I am still.

You are not stuck. You are unwilling.

I push the words out of my head. I don't want to hear them right now. I don't want another reminder that I need to forgive my mother. My chest hurts at the thought.

Mandy sits beside me.

"Why do I always have to forgive?" I mutter. "Why do You always work on me, God? Why not work on her?"

Mandy picks up a rock and tosses it up in the air, catching it again.

She waits. We know how our conversations usually unfold—slowly. We listen, we share, we pray.

"A couple of weeks ago, I came close to cutting myself again," I admit.

The rock Mandy is tossing falls to the ground with a thud.

"I went to see Tammy about it right away. I haven't felt an urge to cut since then, but it was so strong, Mandy. The hurt in my heart was so strong over losing Ben that my body just wanted to let out the pain the old way."

I wish tears would come, but I don't have any left. Whether I ran out at the wedding shower this afternoon or they don't exist when it comes to Nina, I can't tell.

"I felt isolated and alone all over again. It seemed like everyone was darting away from me as fast as they could. Like I was repellent. The isolation felt so similar to being a teenager, the rejection heavy like a coat. I couldn't breathe. I couldn't hope. I could…"

"…only think about letting it out somehow," Mandy finished for me.

I nod again, thankful that she understands.

"Emma, do you remember the time at the Girls Home when you shoved a pushpin into your arm? Tammy made you take it out, and then she placed a bandaid over your wound. Remember that?"

"Yeah."

"Do you remember what you did once she left?"

I cover my face at the memory. "As soon as she left, I found another pushpin, stuck it in my skin, and rolled the bandaid over top of it."

It's easy to laugh now at how ludicrous that was. Everyone could see the lump on my arm. I fooled no one.

"What did I think I was doing?" I wonder.

"You were telling Tammy the truth in the only way you could. Slapping a bandage on the entry point didn't make the pain go away. The thing that caused you pain was still there and a bandage wasn't going to stop it." She reaches into her purse and pulls out a tube of chapstick. "It didn't then and it won't now."

"What do you mean?"

"You couldn't cut Nina out of your life then, Emma, and you can't do it now."

I stare hard at the sidewalk. Green grass pokes up through a crack in the cement, hope in the midst of difficult circumstances.

"So, you're saying Ben is like that safety pin I pushed back into my arm, that I only put a bandaid over my original rejection from Nina," I say. "Then, when Ben left, the same pain came back. You're saying that my pain over Ben really has more to do with my mother."

Mandy starts to laugh. "Wow, that was very Dr. Martha of you. I wasn't expecting anything quite that deep. I was only trying to say that ignoring Nina isn't the same as forgiving her. But I like what you came up with better!"

"Well, I'm in art classes now," I tease. "Everything has layers of meaning."

"It's true, though, isn't it?"

I brush my hair with my fingers. "Yeah, it is true."

"Do you want to pray?" Mandy holds out her hand.

"Yeah, but let me do the talking."

Mandy nods and closes her eyes.

"Dear God, I'm not stuck. I'm unwilling. I'm unwilling to forgive Nina. Please help me become willing. I thought I forgave her a long time ago, but my emotions are having a hard time catching up. Or maybe what I've learned in art class is true: everything does have layers. Help me let Your love heal this layer of my heart."

Mandy whispers "Amen" and gives me a hug.

I reach down and pocket a rock.

Chapter Twenty-Nine

On the drive home from Calgary, I listened to two straight hours of Dr. Martha. During the show, someone called in about their fear of public speaking. Dr. Martha suggested making eye contact with a few people to help engage your audience. That would be great for me… if I didn't have spotty vision and the beginnings of a fainting spell. How am I going to talk to a group of girls?

"Emma Carmichael is our newest volunteer here at the Home," Tammy says, greeting the girls who have gathered in the Girls Home common room.

A few of the teens glance my way. Some offer curious glances, others ignore me or sit with their arms crossed. It's group discussion time and I'm the new girl in the circle.

Tammy leans forward in her chair. "Emma is an alumni member. You graduated the program…" Her brow wrinkles. "Six years ago."

I feel a few more eyes on me.

"In this circle, we talk about our emotions," Tammy continues. "We explore how we're feeling and talk about what the Bible says regarding those emotions. Each of us has a different story and we are all at different places in our journey. I have asked Emma to share her story with us today."

Tammy looks at me and nods. My hands are sweating. They really should invent an antiperspirant for hands. I'm a bit nervous and pray that I won't have an anxiety attack.

Or a heart attack.

Or a stroke.

"My name used to be Chelsea. My mother named me that. My father wanted to call me Alexis, but my mother won. Chelsea means 'stone.'" I make a face and a few girls giggle. At least it's not some weird name that means 'sorrow' or 'sea plant.' "That was me. I was a rock. A hard stone. There was something beautiful inside me, but no one could unearth it."

I survey the group. It was only a short time ago that Mandy and I sat in these very seats wearing ripped jeans and big-time attitude. I can only hope God's love will reach past the armour these girls are wearing.

"I used to be embarrassed by my story. Some of my friends had really traumatic childhoods, perhaps like some of you. Some were sexually molested and abused beyond description. Some grew up with parents who loved their addictions more than they loved their children. And some were victims of violence. For a long time, I thought my story didn't count, because I never encountered those traumas.

"Everyone has a starting point for their pain. Mine was the day my mother left us. It threw my life into a tailspin. My father buried his disappointment in work and just kind of checked out. My sister found a boyfriend, and that became her obsession. My friends seemed to stop liking me and I was left to myself. All alone."

I brush my hair over my shoulder, trying to brush away the memory of the isolation. The empty house, calls from my dad saying he'd be home late, Natalie slamming the door in my face… I let the past fall to floor.

"About two years after my mom left us, she showed up one day. She had changed, though. I knew it from the instant I hugged her. I had been dreaming of that hug for a very long time, but the moment I wrapped myself around her I knew she was different. Her arms felt heavy, like deadwood. I stopped giving my family hugs that day. Affection was too scary, too telling of what someone was really thinking about me. I refused any hugs from my grandparents, my dad, anyone.

"I thought she had come back for me, but it turned out she only wanted her pearl earrings back. They had been a gift from her! Well, I lied and told her I had flushed them down the toilet. She looked at me and said, 'What a waste.' But I knew she wasn't talking about the pearls. She was talking about me."

A girl with red hair gets up and leaves the circle, hiding her face with her hand. Tammy waves me on and slips out of the group, quietly urging the girl to hear my story.

"I was fairly certain I was dead inside. I was only able to feel two things: numbness and pain. My numbness absorbed all my pain until I couldn't feel anything inside. I knew I didn't want to die, but I wasn't sure I was alive. One day, I accidentally cut my leg while shaving. I became fascinated by the blood that bloomed to the surface. Here was proof that I was alive—blood. My blood. After I cut myself, I experienced an emotion I hadn't known in a long time: I was calm. The tranquillity was so foreign to me that I found myself treasuring it. The calmness swept over me and stayed there, keeping me company. And that led to an idea, a resolution to my pain. So, I became a cutter."

I stop to catch my breath. The girl who left the circle is still in the room, just outside the group. Her arms are akimbo, her face stony and hard.

That was me six years ago.

"I put my family through a lot of hell before I ended up here. This was a kind of last resort. It was my rock bottom."

I smile at the rock reference and remind myself to pick one up from the ground before I leave today.

"This place was the best thing God could have done for me. Here, I found friendship and understanding. I didn't have words to explain my reasons for cutting, but the other girls seemed to understand that. My family wanted to know why, but finally my new friends understood me. While I was here, all the childhood truths I had learned became real. I learned about Jesus to find peace in His blood instead of the short-lived calmness from my own.

"As I studied God's word and learned about His heart for me, I realized that I was a new creation in Christ, that Jesus really does make all things new. I then made the decision to make faith in God my own, not just something my family believed. That May, I was baptized and gave a full confession of my love for Him, committing my life to my Saviour. It was on that day that I changed my name to Emerald Carmichael. Jesus' love unearthed the precious gem that was buried inside the stone of my life. He gave me new hope, and I wanted my life to reflect that. I now go by the name Emma, which means 'whole.'

"I don't always feel whole. There are days when I'm a puzzle with half the pieces missing." Tammy and I exchange a look. "But my name, the name God gave me, reminds me of who I am... if I'll listen to it. Every time someone says my name, I'm reminded of who I am and who I belong to. I am whole and new in Christ. I'm precious to Him. I'm no longer a rock, stuck and unmoving. I'm a jewel in the hand of my God."

I look down as I finish my story, finally able to take a deep breath.

Chapter Thirty

"Why don't you create a piece about that time at the retirement home when your wraparound dress came unwrapped?"

"Katie," I say into my cell phone while throwing a suitcase onto my bed. "That won't work as an art project. It's supposed to be meaningful. Not embarrassing."

"You got Guy's number out of it. How is that not meaningful?"

"Guy was an eighty-four-year-old gigolo who walked around with his shirt buttons undone and his orthopaedics hanging out."

"Ew. I forgot about the chest hair."

Katie is no help whatsoever. Typical. I need an art project idea and she wants me to dig through the layers of my most embarrassing moments. As if!

"What am I going to do, Katie? We have to present them next week and I have nothing."

I fold clean clothes into my overnight bag, then hunt for my bridesmaid shoes. I need to leave for Mandy's right after class today if I'm going to make it to the celebration dinner. Debra has asked me to give a toast, and I can't say no; it's Mandy's last night as a single gal.

"Are you anxious about going to Mandy's wedding?"

I press the phone to my ear as I rifle through the bottom of my closet. "Yeah, no, maybe. Look, this is about Mandy. I need to be there for her."

I can practically hear the smile in Katie's voice. "You are going to be okay. You know that, right? You're doing the right thing. I'm so proud of you."

"Stop saying that. You sound like a greeting card."

"I'm allowed. I'm your best friend."

"Well, let's wait until the event is over. I may end up being the bridesmaid who gorges herself on cream puffs and hors d'oeuvres." Which may not be a bad thing if the right hors d'oeuvres are involved.

Katie wishes me luck at the wedding and I say goodbye.

After hanging up, I finally locate the shoes that go with my dress. They're open-toed, which means toenail polish is in order.

I check the clock. There isn't much time, but I'll have to do a quick paint job. There's nothing worse at a wedding than a bridesmaid with tacky toes.

I'm wrong, though. With one phone call, I realize there *is* something worse. Much worse.

———

"It's gone, Emma. My dress is utterly worthless."

Consoling Mandy is a lost cause. There's not much you can say about a bridal shop burning down. A few expletives come to mind, but that won't really help the situation.

"They were supposed to steam the dress, not vaporize it!" Mandy is close to hyperventilating.

I almost say that the store didn't burn down on purpose, but I keep my mouth shut.

"Em, I need you here. Greg tells me he doesn't care what I wear as long as we get married. My mom and Debra are going into hyperdrive. My mom is searching the attic for her wedding gown."

"That doesn't sound so bad."

"She got married in the eighties. One of the sleeves could be a dress all by itself. I can't do this right now. It's too much, Em. I'm supposed to get married tomorrow night! I should have picked up the dress and steamed it myself. I knew it. This is my fault—"

"Mandy, it's going to be okay." The plan is out of my mouth before I have a chance to consider the ramifications. "You can wear my wedding dress."

The phone is silent. Perhaps Mandy has finally passed out from the stress.

"Em, that's your dress."

"No, Mandy. It's yours. You tried it on first, remember? It fits. And you look gorgeous in it." I squeeze my eyes tight. "I certainly don't need it. Please, it's yours."

I hear a sound from Mandy that I've never heard before. It almost sounds like crying. "Emma, thank you. You don't know what this means to me."

I stare at the coffee table. There, sitting in a haphazard pile, is the small collection of rocks I've gathered in the last few weeks. "I have some idea," I manage.

We say our goodbyes and I promise to leave for Calgary in an hour.

I have two things to do after cancelling art class with Andrea. One: see if the Blushing Bride still has my dress. Two: make a long-distance call to Nicaragua and the Bank of Daddy.

Chapter Thirty-One

Chocolate and mint aren't the cure I once believed they were. Two bowls of ice cream from Mandy's supply has done nothing to make me feel safe about attending a wedding tomorrow. Clad in Mickey Mouse jogging pants and an old t-shirt, I climb out of the guest bed at Mandy's parents' house.

I creep over to my suitcase and unzip it quietly.

Debra is snoring on the other side of the bed, earplugs nestled in tightly, a sleep mask pulled over her face. Now I know why the other cousins giggled when I won the coin toss to share a room with Debra. Her snoring could wake the dead.

I had a feeling I would need this—a last-minute stowaway item I threw into my suitcase. Reverently, I remove a large brown hoodie. My face is buried in it before it's all the way out.

Ah, the smell of safety.

The smell of Ben.

I'm nose-deep in the armpit of this sweater, but I don't care. Every once in a while, when I'm lonely enough, I put these sweater arms around me in a semi-embrace. It's pathetic, yes, but it's a step up from the day Natalie found me with it less than a week past my wedding date. I was in my yellow dress attempting to waltz to a Steven Curtis Chapman song. I hadn't showered in two days. It wasn't pretty.

After that, Natalie decided the sweater should stay in a box, hidden in the closet. And it does stay in the closet—except on nights when I can't sleep and need someone to hold on to.

Somehow I knew that I would be needing this tonight. Sinking back onto the pillows, I wrap the hoodie around me.

Mandy looked radiant sitting next to Greg at the rehearsal dinner, listening to all those beautiful words spoken about their love, their teamwork, the difference they make in everyone's lives. Greg then quoted an e.e. cummings poem, eyes filled with love for his bride.

The sting of Ben's absence fills me all over again. I miss him. God, how I miss that man. I don't want to wish away my memories this time. I let them come.

Ben has brown eyes to make chocolate jealous, but he's an awful cook. He could burn water. Once, early in our relationship, he tried to cook chicken wings. We spent our fourth date becoming friends with the local firemen who rescued Ben's kitchen from disaster. He took me out for a strawberry milkshake and donairs afterwards. That became *our* meal.

He has an innate sense of where he is at all times and can find anybody in a store. I've wondered if he has some secret spy training under his belt. Seriously, it's freaky how he just shows up out of nowhere. He also looks really good after he's played football with the boys. Ben in a grey T-shirt has me thinking some unholy thoughts.

Sorry, Jesus.

I toss and turn, wrapped up in the hoodie... wrapped up in Ben. It's a second skin, of sorts. Ben made me feel safe.

Let me be Your shelter. Find refuge in Me.

Burying my head under the sleeve of the arm is the only way to avoid what God is asking me to do. I have to let go of the idea that Ben is my only refuge. How can a piece of fabric become a symbol of idolatry? How come this hurts so much?

When the tears come, I tell myself it's from the fumes wafting off Debra's Vaseline-coated hands.

If only it were that.

It's Ben. It's always Ben. His eyes, his presence, his voice.

Take refuge in Me.

I wrap the sweater even tighter around me. I'm not ready to let go.

The phone rings. Debra snorts but remains asleep.

I stumble to find my cell phone. The clock reads 1:00 a.m.

"Hello?" I answer.

"Emma, please come quickly."

"Andrea? What's wrong? Where are you?"

"I'm in Calgary."

"What?" I shriek, waking up Debra. "Why?"

"Mom's had a heart attack."

I drive to the Foothills Hospital in record time, saying feverish prayers the whole way. I half-run, half-walk to the desk. Before I can ask where my Aunt Cindy is, Andrea calls my name. I turn around and receive a Jack-like attack from her. She grabs me around the neck in a fierce hug.

"It's okay. It's going to be okay." I let her hang onto me, but I'm careful not to let her snot all over Ben's hoodie. If I end up having to wash it, it'll lose his scent. "Let's sit down. What happened?"

We walk over to a set of uncomfortable plastic chairs.

"I don't know. I don't know." Andrea shakes her head. Her arms cross in front of her and tears slip down her face unheeded. "What if I was too late? What if—"

I pull her to my side, rocking her back and forth and stroking her hair. "Shhhh… it's okay."

"I was in my bedroom, Emma, watching a stupid anime movie. She called my name a few times. I just ignored her because it was at the part where the heroine is rescued, and all I could think about was how much I wanted to see the hero kiss the girl."

"You didn't know," I offer.

Andrea sobs. "I finally went to the bathroom to get my curling iron so I could copy the heroine's hairdo. And there was Mom, Emma. Slumped against the door, saying, 'Andrea, help me, help me.'"

I close my eyes and think about how scared Andrea must have felt.

"She was so grey. That's not how I want to remember my mom." Andrea struggles to stay calm. "We went to the Lethbridge Hospital and they transported her to Calgary. She needs some sort of surgery. What if she dies, Emma?"

I look around for Uncle Fred. "Andrea, where's your dad?"

She mumbles something into my hair. I pull back and look at her.

"Where's Uncle Fred?" I repeat.

"He's in Vancouver on business again." Andrea just looks at me. "I haven't called him."

I may have a heart attack of my own. "You haven't called him?"

"It's all my fault. I can't tell him." Fresh sobs wrack Andrea's body. "That's why I haven't called anyone. But I'm scared now, Emma. What if she dies and it's all my fault?"

"You have to tell him, Andrea. This is your dad."

She shakes her head, bent over from shame she shouldn't be feeling.

"Give me your phone." I watch as she presses speed dial 8. Who are the first seven names and why isn't her dad number one?

I'm mentally preparing a voicemail message when Uncle Fred answers the phone.

"Uncle Fred?"

"Who is this?" His voice is gruff with sleep.

"Uncle Fred, it's me. Emma."

Silence greets me. Then, just as suddenly, "What's happened? Is it Papa? Gigi?"

I look around the room, hoping to find some inspiration for how to break the bad news. "Cindy's had a heart attack. Andrea found her and called 911. Lethbridge sent her to Calgary. We're at the Foothills awaiting surgery."

I wait for a response.

"Uncle Fred?"

"Where's Andrea?"

"With me. She's pretty shaken up. Would you like to talk to her?"

Andrea shakes her head.

"Please," Uncle Fred says.

I practically arm-wrestle Andrea into taking the call. I finally have to press the phone to her ear.

"Hello?" she says. Andrea nods her head as she hears her dad's voice. Tears continue to wash down her face as she grips the phone. "I love you, too, Daddy."

The phone drops to her lap when the call ends. Her nose runs as she looks at me with wide eyes.

I pull her into a hug and let her cry all over Ben's hoodie.

Chapter Thirty-Two

Hospital coffee can best be described with a word no good Christian girl should use. This particular brand is strong enough to strip the enamel off your teeth. I'm only drinking it because it gives me the staying power I need in order to remain awake.

"This coffee is—"

I hold up a hand to stop the words from coming out of Uncle Fred's mouth. He arrived an hour ago, while I was nursing my third cup of sewage.

My cell phone chimes, announcing a text. "Uncle Fred, Natalie says Mark is bringing Gigi and Papa. They want to see Aunt Cindy before her bypass surgery this afternoon."

"I'm glad Natalie called them." Uncle Fred rubs his forehead, still looking dishevelled from the red-eye flight from Vancouver. It's only 8:00 a.m., but it feels like it's been a month since Andrea called me from the hospital.

He lifts the coffee cup to his mouth, then decides against it.

"Why don't I go and get us some real stuff?" I want to do something helpful before I leave for my updo appointment in five hours.

"Would you?" Uncle Fred looks at me hopefully. "I could use a double cream, no sugar coffee from Timmy's. How about you, Andi?"

Andrea's eyes warm. Whether it's over the use of the nickname or the thought of hot chocolate, I can't tell.

"Yeah, I'd like that," she says.

Should I take Andrea with me? The suggestion is gone from my mind as Andrea finally sits next to her dad and leans her head against his shoulder.

"I'll be back before you have a chance to miss me," I tell them.

Andrea rolls her eyes, proof that she might be returning to her old self.

I walk towards the elevators, push the down button, and eye the evil coffee machine with disdain.

The elevator doors ding open and I move to go in. Only I can't.

Because my mother is walking out.

"How's Cindy?" she demands, coming straight to the point. As usual. No "Hello." No "How are you?" No pleasantries at all.

I can think of all sorts of weird things—Yeti sightings, cheese in a can, and bagel-head body modification—but my mother standing in front of me in the hospital defies all strangeness.

She sniffs in disapproval over my jogging pants.

"Hey there," I say, studying my pants self-consciously.

"Cindy. Where is she?"

"How did you find out?"

She walks past me, refusing to explain herself, and stops in front of Uncle Fred.

He manages to look up, his head in his hands. "Nina, what are you doing here?"

"Thanks for calling and letting me know my sister had a heart attack." Her voice drips with sarcasm.

Uncle Fred and I exchange a look. Neither of us thought to call her. Gigi and Papa just learned about it, so it couldn't have been them. That leaves Natalie.

The three cups of sludge I drank are taking over for my brain, so I start talking. "Uncle Fred has a lot of other things on his mind. You aren't the first person to come to mind when tragedy strikes."

Nina ignores me completely. "Well, how is she?"

"She's resting," Uncle Fred says. "They're prepping her for bypass surgery later today."

My mother purses her lips.

"Why don't I buy you a coffee?" I offer, exchanging a look with my uncle.

He fishes out a loonie and hands it to me. "Let me treat. You've driven all this way, Nina. It's the least I can do."

I leave them to talk.

Andrea joins me at the coffee machine. "I thought you and Dad said this stuff could remove rust from cars."

"Yep," I say as I push the loonie into the slot. The machine kicks to life.

Andrea chuckles. "You guys are mean."

"You gonna snitch?"

"Are you kidding me?" She pulls out her phone. "I'm gonna get this on video."

———

An hour later, my mother is ready to leave. She saw Aunt Cindy with her own eyes, grilled the doctors about their care, and accused Uncle Fred and me of poisoning her.

But before she leaves, I want answers. Maybe I'm emboldened by the crap coffee I've been drinking all morning.

"I don't understand what you're doing here," I say, catching up to her as she heads to the elevator.

Nina looks at me blankly. "She's my sister, Chelsea. Of course I came."

My heart sinks. "You would come for her, but not for me."

"I don't know what you're talking about, Chelsea."

"Emma, Mom. My name is Emma." We step into the elevator when the doors open.

"Ridiculous name."

"So are those shoes with that bag." I try to blink away my tears. It doesn't work. The tears only come quicker.

My mother once again casts an eye at my Mickey Mouse pants and Ben's oversized hoodie. "I'll try not to be offended."

She is cold, removed. I'm tired of being left out of her world. Everyone tells me I can't bulldoze in, but who's here to stop me now?

"Why haven't you ever come for me, Mom?"

Nina straightens her back.

"I'm talking to you, Mom. I've needed you. Aunt Cindy may have had a heart attack, but I've had a broken heart. Where have you been? You know I didn't get married."

The elevator doors open with a ding. Nina's high heels clip the floor as she pushes past me.

I chase after her. "I'm not done talking, Mother."

She stops only long enough to give me a steely look. "Pull yourself together, Chelsea. You're making a scene."

"Good!" I move my face close to hers. She looks like Natalie, only older, with no kindness in her eyes. "I want to make a scene. Maybe you'll notice me then."

"I have to get back to work. I don't have time for this."

"Say what you mean. You don't have time for *me*."

Nina looks at her watch. "You're right. I don't have time for you."

My mother walks away.

I pull my car keys from my pocket, pressing the edges deep into the palm of my hand.

———

"You're listening to the Dr. Martha Show. My name is Dr. Martha and I'm taking your calls. Next on the line we have Emma from Lethbridge. Welcome to the show, Emma."

With shaking hands, I press the cell phone against my ear. The siren of a fire engine whizzing past drowns out Dr. Martha's voice. I should hang up and leave my parked car. The tall grass on the side of the road waves in the wind, inviting me to come play.

My phone beeps and I see the low battery icon flashing. I should hang up.

"Emma?" Dr. Martha's voice pulls me back.

"I'm here. Thanks for taking my call, Dr. Martha."

"How are you today, Emma?"

"I'm despondent."

"Can you tell me what's going on?"

What am I doing? *Just hang up, Emma. Go home and take up knitting.*

"I want to stop hurting myself." My words come out with a choking sob.

"Okay. Tell me about that," Dr. Martha probes gently.

"I used to self-injure. But that's over now. I don't do that anymore. I haven't for a long time."

Silence swallows up my previous words and I wonder if anyone is driving in their car wondering if my real name is Emma.

"How are you hurting yourself now?"

Why didn't you install a shut-off valve for tears, God? I taste salt as I say the word, "Love."

"I'm sorry, Emma, I can tell you're upset, but I didn't hear that very well. Did you say 'love'?"

I nod. Not that my bobbing head is any indication to Dr. Martha. "Yes. Love. It hurts too much to love sometimes."

"Who does it hurt to love, Emma?"

"I don't know," I say with a shrug. "Everyone. Myself. God." I take a deep breath. "My mother."

"Tell me about her, Emma."

"There's not much to tell."

"I think there is. She wouldn't be on your mind if there was nothing to say. Go ahead, tell me about her."

There's still time to hang up. No shame in that. "She left me. She left me when I was young and she continues to leave me. She didn't see me for three years. No contact, nothing. When I was younger, I thought that maybe, if I was good enough, she'd come back. But I'm not enough. I'm never enough for her." Losing my train of thought, everything tumbles out. "She wasn't even willing to come to my wedding. Not that it matters, though. My fiancé dumped me a few days before the wedding. Even though I have great friends and a family who supported me, all I wanted was my mom. Can you believe that? Still, after everything, after all the ways she threw me to the side, I still wanted her."

The pain in my chest that comes from this admission is agonizing.

"My aunt just had a heart attack and my mom drove in to see her immediately. She dropped everything just to come and see if her sister was okay. I didn't even get a phone call when my fiancé broke my heart. She didn't even take the time to meet him or respond to my wedding invite. How can she just drop everything to see her sister, but not even pick up a phone to call me? What's wrong with me, Dr. Martha? What makes me so unlovable? Why am I so easy to reject? Why is it so easy to walk away from me?"

I'm crying too hard to hear anything Dr. Martha says. The phone utters a beep akin to a death rattle. The screen goes blank. My phone is dead.

I bang my head against the steering wheel twice. After all this time, could that be the reason? Is it because I'm easy to reject? I am unlovable.

Pushing the car door open, I take off into the field, running through the outstretched arms of bending grass. I pump my arms hard, until the ache in my chest is no longer distinguishable from the physical ache of trying to get air into my lungs.

Then I collapse.

The sky above me is blue and the clouds are stretched thin and flat. The wind will be picking up soon—the clouds tell me so.

The ground is hard and I am being stretched thin and flat by my mother's continuous dismissal of me. Who cares if there are burrs in the grass and they get tangled in my hair? I'll chop it off if need be.

People do that when they're shamed, don't they?

They pulled Jesus' beard out. They put a prickly crown on His head. How are we any different?

Father, forgive them, for they know not what they do.

The voice of my slain King echoes deep in my spirit and forces the remaining pain up and out of my mouth. I cry, unashamed. He and I are so different. He is able to do what I cannot.

Sobs wrack my body as all the ways I've felt abandoned by my mother return to me. The memories are strong and vivid.

I pray for the strength to say what comes next. It hurts to speak.

"I forgive Nina, Lord. I forgive my mother for rejecting me. All I've wanted to be was her daughter," I ugly-cry as I utter the words, "but I lay that down. I forgive her for denying me that. What she has said, what she has done, matters. God, I forgive her. I'm sorry for holding her sins against her. Please forgive me, Lord, and all the anger and bitterness I've held towards her." My mouth holds a mix of dust and salt. "Show me Your truth, Lord. What is the truth?"

Wiping my tears, I sit up and wait. The wind moves through the field, swaying the grass on its way to blowing over my face.

You are worthy of love.

I fall back flat.

You are worthy of My love.

It's too good to be true. Christ's rejection makes me worthy, makes me acceptable.

I gather my courage and say, "I am worthy of love."

Speaking the truth out loud frees me to receive all He has for me. I understand His earlier requests for me to build an altar. God doesn't want me to pick up rocks and construct a literal monument. It's about letting Him love me to the deepest parts.

In return, He wants my love. He wants my worship, my broken-and-woundedville worship.

I lift up my voice: "I am loved by You! Creator of the universe, Maker of heaven and earth, Lord of all and King of my heart, I am loved with a love so fierce that it split eternity in two. Time marches around the death and resurrection of your brave act of love. My beloved King, nothing sounds sweeter than the love song you sang to me on the cross. I am forgiven! I am loved! You are holy and You are worthy."

I roll over until the smell of dirt is distinct and pebbles press into my forehead.

"I am loved. I am loved. I *am* loved."

God's presence wraps me in safe arms. His love blots out the lie that says I am easy to reject. I am loved by Him. He's right; the great exchange is His love. My ashes, His beauty.

I am *His* daughter.

And it is enough.

Chapter Thirty-Three

Nothing brings you to the reality of having confessed your life's secrets on national radio like a ton of cell phone messages. Plugged into the wall at the hair salon, my charger brings my dead phone to life.

"Emma, Aunt Cindy here." I gasp. She's supposed to be resting. "A little birdie told me you were on the radio today. Apparently your phone call moved half of North America. I want to cover your story in the magazine. This is big, Emma. Big! Call me."

Beep. Um, okay. How did she hear about that?

"Emma, it's Andrea. My mom stole my cell phone. Sorry she's hassling you. Em, I had no idea you felt that way. That's how I feel most of the time. I love you, Emma, even if no one else does. I do. And there's a male nurse at the front desk who is swearing lifelong devotion as well. But he's also a fan of heavy metal, so I don't see a future for you there. Anyway, Gigi said that we're going to have family prayer at the hospital once they arrive. I'll pray for you, okay?"

Beep. Wait. Andrea… praying?

"It's Natalie. Mark, Gigi, and Papa all heard the call on the drive to the hospital and told me about it. We're going to sit down and have a talk about this. Seriously, Emma, please know that you are loved. We love you. I love you. Call me. Please take care of yourself and call me."

Beep. Same old Nat, motherly as ever.

"Emma, Mrs. MacDonald here." Ugh, did Natalie share my cell phone number with *everyone?* "I just listened to your radio call off the link on your sister's blog. There is someone who loves you, Emma. Mr. MacDonald is the epitome of true devotion. See, you are needed. Speaking of which, he needs his toenails clipped. What are you doing Monday? Toodles."

Beep. Ugh!

"Emma, it's Tammy. The girls and I listened to your call to Dr. Martha while we were driving in the van to the waterpark. It started a huge outpouring of love over here at the Girls Home. Some of the girls are finally talking about stuff that has taken them weeks to open up about. We all love you, Emma. We are here for you."

Beep. I guess God's turning this humiliation around for me. Only He has that kind of power.

"Emma! This is Katie. Pick up. Pick up now. I heard you on the radio today. Pick this phone up and call me. Now! I love you, Em. You are my best friend and you are going to be okay. Call me, okay?"

Tears spring to my eyes at the outpouring of love. It is very unexpected, but not unwelcome.

I am loved.

Beep.

Voice mailbox full.

————

Country music is being piped through the hotel bathroom speakers. With the wedding starting here in an hour, it's a relief to realize that I'm starting to heal. Not every country song defines me. I know, for sure, that I'm not a red-necked woman.

My stomach rumbles. Yogurt with fruit may not have been the best choice for a quick snack, but who can order steak when you're squeezing in a hair appointment and a personal meltdown on national radio mere hours before a wedding?

My cell phone chirps and announces that Aunt Cindy is going into surgery within the hour. I say a quick prayer.

"My date cancelled on me," Debra says from her position in front of the mirror next to me. She's putting on lipstick, or at least trying to; she'll get the lipstick close to her mouth, then pull it away and start talking animatedly. She does it over and over again. "He cancelled on me! Can you believe it?"

Shocker.

"That's too bad," I say, adjusting the flower in my hair.

"His lame excuse was that he forgot his band was committed to play for some men's retreat this weekend."

I nod silently as Debra's lipstick hovers close to her lips. She's going to do it this time, I think. But no, she starts yapping again.

"I know! I can't believe it, either. But it's fine. I'm just going to dance with one of Greg's single guy friends."

I suppress a snort. I've hung out with Greg long enough to know his single guy friends—and they're all single for a reason.

"Who knows," she says, "maybe I'll meet my future husband here at Greg and Mandy's wedding."

I practice my grin in the mirror. We'll be taking a gazillion pictures today and I want to make sure my smile looks genuine. Not too forced.

Debra only takes this smile to mean I think meeting her future husband is an actual possibility. Maybe it is. Stranger things have happened, as I know all too well after this morning.

———

Mandy is all about bright pink. The bouquets are made of stargazer lilies. The runner is bright pink. Mandy's hair is bright pink, too, flipped out at the tips. You wouldn't think a bride could pull off such outrageous hair with a traditional Cinderella gown, but Mandy can.

We're all standing around her in our black dresses, admiring her in my—no, correction—*her* gown.

My stomach feels queasy and my gut churns. My growing anxiety falls off with a shrug and in my heart I know that I'm happy she's wearing this gown.

The other girls giggle. "Mandy, you look amazing! Greg is going to freak."

"Or cry!"

"Or run up the aisle to get you."

Mandy takes a deep breath and smooths her gown. Her arms no longer carry the same scars. Her three deepest cuts have been covered with a tattoo that reads "Love never fails."

The doors to the ballroom are closed, but we can hear music through the door.

"The mothers are about to light the candles," Debra says, wringing her hands. She tries to peek through the crack in the door. Now would be a bad moment for someone to swing the door open into her face. But maybe it'd solve her snoring problem?

Debra steps back. "I don't want to alarm you, and we definitely don't want to alarm Mandy, but..." She looks over both her shoulders to make sure Mandy can't hear. "Both of our groomsmen are M.I.A."

"Are you sure about this?" I ask, my stomach flipping at the possibility of heading down the aisle by myself. "Where are they?"

"I saw Greg a few minutes ago. He said that he got a text from them. They're stuck in traffic. Apparently some train is stopped on the tracks and cars are backed up for a mile."

My stomach drops again. "What are we going to do? Are we going solo?"

"Emma!" Debra hisses. "We've been over this. The groomsmen are going to escort the bridesmaids down the aisle—dancing. It's just a two-step shuffle. Remember? We aren't abandoning the dream because of some train." Debra licks her lips and straightens her shoulders. "I sent my mother to find two guys in similar suits from among the guests. It'll work out."

"Couldn't we just go solo?" I offer.

I now know how a mouse feels right before it's eaten by a snake.

"I'm *not* walking down that aisle by myself, okay?" Debra says. "I may be the older, unmarried cousin, but I will not be without an escort."

"Okay." Checking over my shoulder, Mandy is behind us and oblivious to what is going on.

Everyone takes their places in line behind the flower girls. As the wedding coordinator gives us a litany of last-minute instructions, I look around for our replacement groomsmen. Where are they? I can't see anyone. I'll probably get one of Greg's single friends, someone who plays online video games and smells like dill pickle chips. Just the thought makes me want to gag.

If they don't show up, does that mean I'm going to be a solo act heading down the aisle? My hands start to sweat. Should I bob and sway to keep up the dance theme, or just walk? Will I be expected to do more dance moves since my partner is missing? A disco strut? A mambo?

Suddenly, I hear the start of orchestral music. The doors open just as Bing Crosby's voice croons out, "Mandy, there's a minister handy..."

I'm working on my first move when my partner steps beside me. Without looking, I say, "It's about time. I was about to go solo. Nobody wants to see me do the splits."

I hear a chuckle that covers me like fairy dust. For a moment I feel happy, certain that I'm going to lift off the ground.

Then dread overcomes me—because I recognize that laugh.

My escort is Ben.

Chapter Thirty-Four

When overcome with shock, notable women in history have had a myriad of responses. Some drop their jaws with a tell-tale catch in their breathing. Others bring their hands to their face. Others faint. Still others rise above the embarrassment of the moment, turn swiftly, and put on an air that says, "I was quite certain this was going to happen and I'm very pleased to see that I've proven myself right."

My reaction is to freeze.

And then I throw up a little. In my mouth.

Seeing as I have to dance down the aisle right at that moment, I can't spit it out, leaving me with the horrible choice of swallowing it back down and plastering a grin on my face. I link arms with Ben and start a two-step shuffle.

Are we dancing like a superstar couple? No clue. I am preoccupied with the fact that spit-up lingers in my mouth. Oh yeah, and the love of my life is dancing me down the aisle, ushering me into a wedding.

A wedding that is not ours.

I have a new respect and appreciation for Job, from the Bible. Perhaps he and I alone could ask the question, "When will the humiliation end?"

Ben leans over as we pass the first two rows. "You look beautiful, Emma."

My name. He said *my* name.

I smile at him. Not because I want to, but because I will not talk to him with puke-breath. The man hasn't seen me in four months. His memory of seeing me again for the first time isn't going to be tinged with stomach acid.

"Are you okay?" he whispers. "You look really shocked. I'm sorry… I didn't plan this."

His words are cut off as an elderly lady stands up and snaps our picture. She got me mid-blink.

Ben and I reach the front of the aisle and I expect to walk to the bride's side. But Ben's arm holds me fast. I look up at him. He motions with his head over to the groom's side, and then I remember: Mandy wants us standing as couples on the stage. Two on the right, two on the left.

But I can't think about that now. My stomach is executing the movements of a triple-loop rollercoaster. As a previous victim of food poisoning, I'm blaming the lemon and pomegranate yogurt. Maybe that wasn't bits of lemon rind I was eating.

Debra looks at me and whispers, "Em, are you okay? You look like a zombie. Really, you look awful."

I shake my head and Debra whispers something to Ben. They start a quick conversation while casting glances at the side door.

Thank goodness the guests are looking towards the back of the aisle, craning their necks for a peek at Mandy. It's for the best; I may toss my cookies and it's better if no one is there to catch them.

Suddenly, the moment for Mandy's entrance arrives and everyone stands.

My gut churns as the taste of bile rises to the back of my throat. I eye the purse hanging over Greg's grandmother's shoulder. It looks big enough to hold the contents of my stomach. But how does one steal an elderly woman's handbag without drawing attention from everyone?

Ben's arm tugs me gently away from the platform towards the side door. I try to stay, but I can't. I have two options: leave and throw up in a hallway plant, or stay and ruin Mandy's pink wedding.

My feet move towards the side door. I have just enough time to see Mandy's beaming face, her eyes locked with Greg and her dress radiant.

Ben pulls me out into the hallway. The air is refreshingly cool out here, but not cool enough to prevent my body from doing what needs to be done.

Ben stands in front of me and grabs my shoulders. "Emma, are you okay?"

I look up at him in time to say "Sorry."

And then I throw up all over him.

———

"I think I puked up the gastronomic equivalent of all the anxiety I've felt over the last four months, Nat."

I can hear Natalie trying not to laugh. "But are you okay?"

"Yeah," I say into my cell phone as she starts to giggle. "It's not funny."

"It will be one day."

"Says the sister who blogs my life instead of her own."

Natalie ignores my comment. "What are you going to do, Emma? You need to lie down somewhere. Food poisoning is serious."

"The hotel put me in this side room to wait until the wedding is over. But I've pretty much just been hanging out in the bathroom. All my clothes are at Mandy's house, so I can't change. Don't worry, I'll think of something."

"Right," Natalie says with little confidence. "I'll try and think of something."

I end the call and wonder how the ceremony is going, and if it's almost over. Will Mandy laugh joyously when she says her vows? Will Greg speak his vows in the iambic pentameter, like he threatened to?

Clutching my stomach, I manage to wobble to the doorway. After I threw up the first time, I told Ben to change his clothes. He tried to follow me into the ladies bathroom, but I wouldn't let him. I also told him that he stunk.

That felt good.

Actually, throwing up all over him was okay, too. My mind may have failed to give me the correct response to seeing him, but my body sure came through.

Sorry, Jesus. I really should feel terrible about throwing up all over him. And I do. A little bit.

"Emma!"

Leaning against the door for support, I give a small wave to Mandy.

"Are you okay?" She doesn't wait for an answer but marches me back to the sofa and makes me sit down.

"I'm sorry I missed out on your big day. I missed it, Mandy. I'm so sorry."

Mandy bites her lip. "Em, I didn't even notice you were gone until the photographer said we would be taking photos in ten minutes. I just found out. I was so happy to finally stand beside Greg that I tuned everything else out."

I wheeze out a laugh.

"But you were with me the whole time, Emma. Even if it was just in the form of this dress." She pulls at the skirt. "My wedding is such a fiasco. First the wedding dress shop burns down, then you get sick, the groomsmen show up late... Oh, Emma—Ben! I saw it all happen at the last second. I didn't even know he was here. He said he wasn't coming to the wedding. Are you okay? Where is he?"

"I threw up on him."

Mandy stares in shock. "You didn't."

"I certainly did."

Mandy and I share a knowing look, then burst out laughing again.

"I don't even know what to say about that," she says.

"Neither do I."

Before we can launch into a third round of laughter, Debra's voice interrupts our friendly chatter. "Mandy, it's picture time."

"I can't leave you here like this." Mandy crosses her arms and tilts her head.

I pause for a moment, thinking her statement over. Our friendship ended up running deeper than any cut our blades could make. It brought us through rough waters. It brought us here.

"You can leave me," I say, knowing that it's okay to let people go.

Mandy thanks me and heads back to her new husband's side. I watch her dress and train follow behind her out the door.

I close my eyes and try to calm my stomach. "I trust You, God. I trust You with whatever it is You have next for me," I whisper.

I may have spoken too soon.

"Here she is." Debra's voice grates into my meditations. I peek open one eye and see Debra looking over me. "Come on, Emma. Your ride is here."

My gaze travels from Debra to my ride—to my mother.

Chapter Thirty-Five

My mother is dressed in a white pantsuit with Manolo heels. "I love your shoes," I say.

"I got them in New York this spring. I bought them for a wedding."

My wedding, I hope. I push down the thought. "I don't think you should drive me anywhere. I'm not feeling well. I don't want to ruin your car if I... you know..."

I gesture to my stomach so she understands that I'm talking about puking—or in her case, vomit. Actually, I don't even know if she's ever talked about throwing up. She doesn't seem like the type.

She juts out her chin. I'm beginning to understand that she does this when she's thinking.

"Stay here," she says. "I'll be right back."

I think about Ben. I mean, really *think* about him. He was here, beside me, and I threw up on him.

What does it all mean? Why is my mother even here? Then I know. This is Natalie's doing.

I hear the distinctive sound of her heels returning to me. "Get up, Buttercup."

We stare at each other in shock. That's how she would wake me up every morning when I was little. I loved to sleep then, too. She used to shake me awake with those endearments.

She looks equally surprised that they fell out of her mouth.

"Where are we going?" I ask shakily, standing up and smoothing my dress.

My mother holds up a plastic card with a bemused expression. "The executive suite. Where else?"

I narrowly survive the elevator ride, managing to contain myself right up until I get to the suite's bathroom. Staring into the mirror, I contemplate the last two hours of my life with rare diffidence. My wedding dress gets to the altar before I do, Ben shows up, my mother rescues me, and now I'm hugging a toilet bowl and trying to sit up.

It all seems a bit surreal, like a well-staged reality TV show with bad writers.

A search around the bathroom for hidden cameras proves futile. There are none.

I wash my face and wobble over to the bed. My mother is on her cell, explaining to someone that she wants to reschedule her plans for the evening. For me? I can't hope for it. It seems too big. Too impossible.

The banner hanging in the church in Montana comes back to me: *"Never let your memories be greater than your dreams."* What was the dream for my mother and me? I don't even know anymore.

She ends her call and turns to me. "That was Papa. Aunt Cindy just woke up from surgery."

"Just now?" The pieces fall in place. My mother could have stayed at the hospital to be there for Aunt Cindy, but she came here.

"I don't know what to do with you," she says finally.

I blink. How do I answer that? With a hug?

A knock sounds at the door, annoying my mother. I sit up and watch as she crosses the room to answer it.

She's here. She came. I'm in trouble and she came. She got me a room. It's the best gesture of love I've received in a long time.

My mother opens the door slowly.

It's Ben.

"Is Emma here?" he asks.

I can't see my mother's face, only her stance. She looks... protective. "Who are you?"

"I'm Ben."

"Ben?" Her voice carries surprise.

"Can I see her?" Ben sounds eager, worried even. My heart warms.

"No, Ben. You can't see her."

Ben opens his mouth to speak, but my mother cuts him off. "She's not ready to see anyone right now. You can call here tomorrow morning and see if she feels up to it. Right now, she needs her rest."

Ben is about to protest. I assume my mother lasers him with one of her penetrating stares because he quickly thanks her and leaves.

I don't know how to feel, besides sick to my stomach. It's a horrible thing to take one's emotional temperature and find out there's no reading. I haven't felt this confused since I tried to follow the plot of the *Left Behind* movie.

My mother returns to me. I feel small in the bed and want her to take care of me.

And in a way, she just has.

"Let him sweat it out for a day," she says, walking over to her purse and picking it up.

I smile. "Thank you."

She should stay. I need her to stay. The purse in her hands tells me that she has no plans to remain, though. This is all I get. I want more, but this is all she can give right now. In some ways, it is enough. In most ways, it isn't nearly.

"My assistant will come with some medications and clothes. She should be here in a half-hour. If she isn't, please inform me. She's been late once before and I'll not have that being part of my reputation."

I nod in understanding.

Nina looks around the room in that awkward way people do when they know they need to leave but they also know they should stay.

I take my cue. "Mom." I pause for effect. "Thank you."

"Yes, well, don't thank me yet. You haven't slept on the mattress, experienced the room service, or eaten the food. Thank me once all these things prove satisfactory."

The words are inside me. I have to let them out. To forfeit this opportunity would mean letting the words live under my skin.

"No, I mean *thank you*. For coming. Thank you for coming when I needed you."

She looks away, unable to look me in the eyes. "Yes, well, like I said, don't thank me until you try the food."

Her profile is outlined like a silhouette from the days of old. Her blond hair is in a chignon, her nose pointed and straight, her shoulders held back proudly. I then realize the truth: my mother is a stone. She's stuck in a river and life moves around her. She's stuck there because she is unwilling. Unwilling to be loved. Unwilling to be forgiven.

Only love can erode away edges that sharp.

"I love you, Mom."

She continues to stare in the direction of the door. I don't know whether she heard me or not.

"Goodbye, Mom. I'll let you know how the food is."

"Yes, do that." She looks at me quickly, then heads for the door.

I hear it click shut a moment later.

Chapter Thirty-Six

In the mirror, I can see the door my mother just left through. I also see my own reflection, and I look like a sickly child found on those hunger ads they run on television. Physically, I feel awful. Emotionally… well, throwing up is the perfect way to describe the mess of emotions that have dominated my life these last four months. It's a soup of shock, anger, hurt, grief, and a large dose of bitterness. The truth is that none of it can stay inside me. It will poison me if it does.

Feeling dizzy, I make it to the bathroom just in time to empty my guts again.

As soon as I'm finished, there's a knock at the door. My mom's assistant makes good time. I hope Nina asked for fuzzy pyjamas and not some silky Victoria Secret number.

I pull the door open—it's Ben.

"You came back," I say.

He nods. My stomach twists and I can't tell if it's the food poisoning or nerves at seeing him again. He looks good. His black hair is sticking up in that dishevelled yet styled way I just adore. His face shows open concern.

"Excuse me."

I flee to the bathroom in time to close the door and puke. I lie down and rest my head against the tile floor. I start counting the tiles—there are forty-two. The tiles are cold and white. The grout lines are a dingy yellow.

What is Ben doing here? Of all the times to make an appearance, why now? Why show up when I'm the most vulnerable, when I'm in need of being taken care of? What does this mean?

"God," I whisper into the tiles. "I don't understand this moment. Actually, I don't understand this *day*. Please give me some clue here."

Build Me an altar.

I manage a guttural laugh. Even here, on the bathroom floor, with my ex-fiancé standing just outside, God wants me to thank Him. I guess the answer is that none of this is about me, and it never has been. It's about Him. Do I believe He's worthy of honour and praise, even when my life is this messy?

"Yes, Lord. You are worthy. You are good and kind. You are worth all the glory and honour and praise. Now, please, help me. Any chance of an angel showing up with a hairbrush, deodorant, and some Bananca?" I look around the room for a glow of light and a bag of toiletries. "No. Okay, You are still worthy of praise."

I finally creak open the door, hoping that my walk from the sink to the door has allowed for a complete transformation. When I last glimpsed myself in the mirror, I was a red-eyed, pale-faced behemoth. And that's being kind.

Ben is still standing by the door, his hands shoved deep in his pockets like they always are. He remains at the edge of the room, unwilling to walk deeper into my space uninvited. I immediately appreciate him for it.

"You should go," I say. I can't be trusted around him.

His expression is unreadable. He moves towards me with an arm extended, as though he wants to help me walk. I can only think of what it feels like to be held by him.

"I need to be alone right now." I take a step back, then try standing firm in one spot. My knees shake.

Ben drops his arm and runs a hand through his hair in frustration. "I can't leave you like this, Emma."

My minds races with a thousand replies. I'm tempted to say that he had no trouble leaving me before, but it rings petty and hollow in my mind. It would hurt him and hurt any possibility of us having a real conversation.

"You should go. Please." I hope he knows that underneath the words, I'm really asking him to stay.

Ben looks towards the window, then back at me. "Can we sit out on the balcony? The fresh air might make you feel better."

"The heights might make me puke again."

"Just puke over the balcony."

We laugh. It breaks the tension, like the slackening of a rope at the end of a long tug-of-war.

Ben opens the balcony door and arranges a chair for me. He gently lowers me into it and then retrieves a blanket from the room, wrapping it around my shoulders.

His kindness makes my insides quake.

Sitting across from me, Ben moves to take my hands, stopping only when I flinch.

"I'm sorry for surprising you," he says. "I just wanted to see you."

I stare at his wonderful face and try to remind myself that I should be looking at him like he's a spider.

"I heard your call on Dr. Martha, Em."

Jesus, return to earth. Right now. Emergency exit. On the double.

I shrug, attempting to play it cool. "Oh, that."

"I needed to see that you were okay."

I turn and study the Calgary skyline, a million lights coming to life as the sun sets behind the buildings.

"That was your mother, wasn't it?" Ben touches my arm. "It's good that she was here for you. I'm happy for you, Em."

I try to think of something to say, but I can only manage, "Ben, I think I'm going to be sick."

Ben's shoulders slump. "But I need to talk to you."

Am I ready to hear what he has to say? Will he finally tell me the real reason for calling off the wedding? Will those reasons bring closure?

"What is it, Ben?"

He looks at me squarely. "I leave in the morning."

And there it is. The truth. No sugar added. He has no plans of staying and no plans of opening up to me.

I'm angry. Is he here because he's concerned about me? Or because talking to me right now is convenient for him?

I cross my arms in front of me.

Ben sighs. "You're angry."

It takes all my willpower to stop from saying, "No kidding, Captain Obvious!" Instead I just say, "Like I said, I'm sick."

"And angry," Ben adds.

I fight a smile. "And angry." I look at the balcony floor. There's a stain on the patio by Ben's shoes.

He lifts my chin up with his fingers. "Emma."

He breathes out my name and it glides over my cheek. Looking into his eyes, I know what he's thinking, the way I always knew before he left me.

I brush his hand away and go back to staring at the floor. Ben leans in closer. I can smell his spicy soap. I know he can smell my wretched sick smell, too. I want him to be far away from me.

Ben puts his hands in his pockets, controlling his effort to touch me. Maybe he's unsettled by seeing me again. Maybe he doesn't know what to do with his feelings, either.

He was about to tell me that he loves me. I know it.

But none of that matters if he's leaving.

He stands and begins to pace back and forth. I can tell he's after something. Is it a future with me or closure on the past? I'm afraid to ask, but I do anyways.

"Ben, why are you here?"

His gaze is tender and I immediately want to wrap my arms around him and forget every evil thought I ever had about him.

"I came to say goodbye."

My heart stops and I'm not sure I can breathe. He's leaving me... again.

"We didn't get a chance to say goodbye." Ben looks at me sorrowfully. He loves me. I love him. This should be easy math, yet somehow I know—finally know—that the only future I have with him is saying goodbye.

This hurts.

I'm not going to get any answers today. Maybe I never will.

Looking down at my wrinkled dress, now covered with the dust and dirt of the many bathroom floors I've been on, I want to cry. Why couldn't I have been wearing something stunning, my hair brushed and my breath minty? Why couldn't we have said goodbye standing in the rain, like in a country song?

Goodbyes never happen that way. Maybe that's for the best. If they happen when you're messy and dark, there's no room left for romance. I'll always remember this goodbye for what it is: horribly ugly.

Ben is still staring at me. He's torn. He feels awful for doing this right now, yet he wants this to happen before he leaves. I wish he would just *say* these things so I don't have to read between the lines. Is that asking for too much? The truth is, I don't know if he's being kind or selfish. Maybe I don't know him at all. Maybe I never did.

I shut my eyes and feel the wind blow against me. When I finally open my eyes again, I whisper three words, and not the three words I had hoped to be saying: "You should go."

He looks at the floor and nods. "I'm sorry."

I know he is. Something is eating him up inside. He isn't going to tell me why he left. I deserve an answer, but I know he doesn't have one for me. Not today.

I grip the sides of the patio chair. Ben's eyes meet mine as he gently helps me up. For some strange reason, I love him best at this moment.

With one hand on my back, he guides me back inside. He walks towards the door and I shuffle along behind him. The telling creak of the door fills my ears as he pulls on the doorknob.

Hesitating, he faces me one last time. "Do you remember the day you wore that yellow dress?"

I bow my head. "Yes."

"That was a good day."

I nod, tears stinging my eyes.

He reaches out and caresses the side of my face. "Goodbye, Emma. I'm sorry."

"Goodbye, Ben."

The door closes slowly as I watch Ben walk away.

Chapter Thirty-Seven

I get a text from Andrea: *Celebration dinner for Mom at Gigi and Papa's tonight.*

I look up from my art easel and roll my eyes. "I'm right here. You can tell me these things."

Andrea shrugs as she keeps typing: *We're having smoked salmon. It's good for the heart. We're on a healthy heart diet now that Mom is out of surgery and back at home.*

"Again, I'm right beside you. Just talk to me."

No way. Texting is better. Plus, you should see your face when you get a text from me. Ha!

I make a big show of putting my phone away. It beeps a minute later and I give Andrea a saucy look.

The sound of hands clapping brings the room to attention. Our break is nearly over and my palms are beginning to sweat. I'm still unconvinced that I'm doing the right thing. Talking is hard sometimes. Maybe I could text my presentation?

I roll my shoulders and study the mixed media piece in front of me. My neck is still sore from the marathon creative sessions I've pulled the last few days.

When I came home on Sunday, an idea took shape inside me. Then it became an obsession. After that, it was me and glue for the next three days while I laboured over the masterpiece in front of me.

I can still see the grey around the edges, but there's always going to be a bit of grey.

I've made peace with that.

"The first few presentations had a great deal of thought and provocation hidden within the pieces," Monique says. "Mixed media is all about repurposing, finding new uses for old things, taking something that seems worn and forgotten and bringing new life to it."

Monique looks at her clipboard list, then makes eye contact with me.

"Emma, you're next."

I smile weakly. Now would be a good time to run to the bathroom and count the floor tiles. I push the thought away. I can move forward even when I don't want to. If I've learned nothing else, it's *that* simple truth.

I hold the canvas in my hands and head to the front of the class. I hear my cell phone beep from inside my bag. Somehow I don't need to check it to know that Andrea is sending me love.

She's so weird.

With every step I take towards the front of the room, I'm filled with gratitude for the steps that have led me here. I'm grateful for Andrea. I'm grateful for the best friend who ditched her so I could become a poor substitute.

Facing the class, a smile breaks out on my face. I can't help it. I shouldn't be in this place, both literally and figuratively. It was never my plan to be in art class, to dig through layers and find old things and give them new meaning. It was never my plan to be a Restorer of Broken Things.

I clear my throat and hold up the canvas. I have prepared an introduction and I hope I can get through it without my mind going blank.

"They say that art imitates life." I look around the room and meet the curious gazes of a few students. "In this case, I can say that my art has definitely imitated my life. Working on this project helped me give voice to many things, so I'm going to say them. Here. Out loud. Not because you need to hear them, but rather because I need to say them."

I give a quick look to Monique, who nods in approval. Out of the corner of my eye, I see Andrea smiling. I know she'll hear my words. More importantly, *I'll* hear my words.

And God will, too. He's heard it all before, but for some reason I know He wants to hear this story one more time.

I slowly turn my canvas and lift it up onto the easel. I hear a few rustling noises throughout the room. I wonder for a moment what the class is thinking. It doesn't matter, though. It really doesn't.

This is for me. And for Jesus.

"I call this piece 'My Scarred Altar.' It's a self-portrait."

I close my eyes, knowing I've said the words out loud. A few heads nod and I believe they're telling me that they see it. They see me.

"A long time ago, I used to cut myself." On the canvas, I point to a razor blade positioned as my mouth. "I didn't know how to give voice to my thoughts and emotions. But this blade did. It did damage to my skin, reflecting the damage I felt inside. It was how I knew I was alive. It was the only way to get rid of my anxiety and fear and hurt."

I lift up my eyes.

"Before, when I cut myself, it was because I felt so rejected. I felt as though I had no worth to my mother, to my family." I give Andrea a brave smile. "It was a lie then, and it's a lie now. But I didn't remember that until a few days ago."

I take another deep breath and wipe my hands on my pants.

"At the beginning of summer, I was overwhelmed with a new situation that caused me to believe I was someone worth rejecting." I force the words out. "The man I love and planned to marry cancelled our wedding a few days before the big day."

I hear soft gasps. The guy who chews bubble gum makes a loud popping sound as a bubble explodes.

"I was rejected and bruised. Damaged. I became afraid. Losing Ben dropped me into such a dark hole that I felt..." I pause, searching for the right word. Splayed? Gutted? Severed? "...lost. But I knew that a blade would only take me down darker a hole.

"I'm a Christian, so I prayed. I prayed for strength, for help, for a way to stop being dark. As I prayed, I thought about Jesus. He was whipped, beaten, tortured, and forced to wear a crown of thorns. Nails pierced His hands, scarring Him. The soldiers pierced His side, scarring Him. Jesus was scarred by life so that I could be scarred by His love. I am left with a mark on my soul. He loves me. He knows my pain. He understands my sorrow."

Tears form and I decide to point at the next item on the canvas—a wedding invitation—in an effort to offset them.

"I used the razor to cut this wedding invitation. I also sliced up some of the cards my fiancé gave me while we were dating. These items make up my hair in the collage. The material making up my shirt comes from a yellow dress I own."

I don't tell them the significance of the yellow dress. I also show the keycard from the hotel room my mom got me, but I'm not yet ready to talk about that with anyone.

Maybe I'll tell Natalie tonight at the party. Maybe not.

I start to giggle. "I took this label for chocolate chip mint ice cream and wrestled it into a right angle, turning it into my nose. It represents the many impulsive mistakes I've made from when I was hurt and ran from the pain."

Two sour candies make up my eyes. I've used them to commemorate the day Andrea and I saw my wedding dress in the store window. One of Natalie's blog posts has been cut up and made into a hairband. I've also found unique uses for items representing Katie, Mandy, and all my friends—even little Jack.

"True friends love you in spite of your mistakes. They show up and support you in various ways. My family and friends loved me, even when I was at my lowest."

Next, I point to the printed email Dr. Martha sent me requesting that I call the show again and finish our conversation. I'm slotted to be on the air tomorrow afternoon. I still have no idea what I'm going to say.

"My Papa has always been a source of wisdom for me." I point to the first rock he gave me, the rock that started my restoration. "He told me to remember. He told me to remember God and to remember what He has done for me."

I run my fingers across the small rocks that represent my altar to

God. These are the rocks I've picked up throughout the last few weeks. I'm not going to tell the class the meaning of these rocks. Some things are too precious to share.

I do point out the scriptures I've written on them, though. The first one, which I read aloud, is the scripture Papa wrote on the rock. It's from Exodus 20:24.

"This rock says, *'Build altars in the places where I remind you who I am, and I will come and bless you there.'* I have been learning about knowing God in all sorts of circumstances and receiving the blessing of knowing Him in those moments.

"I coated each rock in several layers of paint. The first rock, as you can see, starts out fully black. I scraped away the paint on each rock, so they form a progression from black to shades of grey, and finally, the last stone emerges as a green emerald. It's a precious stone that has come about after much polishing and buffing. Just like me."

The green stone winks at me. I'm glad I used clear nail polish on it. The rock looks fresh, full of hope. I painted this rock while talking with Tammy on the phone. Bridgeway Home for Girls is starting a fall internship program that runs for eight months, and Tammy wants me to be part of it. There's no pay, but my dad says, *"Mi casa es su casa."* As for spending money, well, something tells me Mr. and Mrs. MacDonald could use some mani-pedis on a regular basis.

I gesture to all the sliced-up, ripped-up, cut-up media that comprises my self-portrait. "This may be a scarred altar, but I'm loved with an everlasting love from my Saviour, Jesus. And somehow, that makes me whole."

I exhale a long breath. I'm done. My hands have finally stopped sweating.

"Thank you, Emma," Monique says. She makes eye contact with me. Together, we have one of those silent conversations in which everything is said through a glance. She says a lot this way, and I hope it stays with me forever.

I take my seat.

"And that is the power of art, class. We can capture a moment or a feeling or," she turns to me and smiles, "a journey."

Her voice fades into the background as I stare at my self-portrait.

I'll still cry myself to sleep some nights. I'm nowhere near to being fully recovered. I still love Ben. That isn't going away, and it won't for a long time. But I have my hands gripped around the truth that sustains me.

I am loved and I am worthy of love. I am God's daughter.

I run my hands over the rocks again, letting them rest on the scripture I wrote onto the rock I picked up last, after talking with Ben:

Daughter, you took a risk of faith, and now you're healed and whole. Live well, live blessed! (Mark 5:34, The Message)

The verse makes me smile.

Because it's true.

CPSIA information can be obtained at www.ICGtesting.com
Printed in the USA
LVOW13s0432221113

362287LV00001B/15/P